The Human Microbes

The Human Microbes

by
Louise Michel

translated, annotated and introduced by
Brian Stableford

A Black Coat Press Book

ISBN 978-1-61227-116-3. First Printing. October 2012. Published by Black Coat Press, an imprint of Hollywood Comics.com, LLC, P.O. Box 17270, Encino, CA 91416.
Printed in the United States of America.

Introduction

Les Microbes humains, here translated as *The Human Microbes*, was first published by Dentu in 1886, not long after Louise Michel's release from jail, where it must have been written. She had been sentenced to six years of solitary confinement in 1883, but was released early by order of the President of the Republic, Jules Grévy, as part of a general amnesty afforded to anarchist prisoners; in the meantime, effectively deprived of oral communication, she had had no refuge but writing. That fact needs to be recorded first and foremost, the context of her imprisonment providing foundations of both the form and context of the narrative, which would otherwise be bordering on the inexplicable. The long and tormented route by which Louise Michel reached that particular prison sentence is also of considerable importance to a full appreciation of the narrative, but it is worth pausing briefly to focus more narrowly on the implication of the raw fact.

Although it was clearly written with publication in mind, that cannot have been the author's primary move for writing the narrative; that primary motive can only have been to help provide a distraction and an internal refuge from her awful circumstances. It was not her first priority during that time, or even her second; her first priority must have been her correspondence; she wrote regularly to her mother, who was in poor health, her friends and her enemies (i.e., the government); her major project during the two years plus of her confinement, however, was writing her memoirs, the first volume of which was also published in 1886. Her novel presumably added some variety to that program, and was almost certainly composed in dribs and drabs, with very few extensive focused stints.

By necessity, therefore, *Les Microbes humains* is the work of an author who was certainly poorly-nourished, by no means in good condition physically, and under very considerable mental stress. It was probably written with poor implements, on paper of poor quality, and certainly without any access to reference books. When the manuscript was eventually handed to the publisher—some years before the author had initially anticipated having that opportunity—it must have posed a difficult challenge.

A fair copy was probably made, from which the typesetter could work, perhaps after the intervention of a copy-editor, but making that fair copy must have been a challenging task, and the internal evidence suggests that it was not done by the author; nor did the author check the proofs. In all probability, she was far too busy, not only in attending to her ailing mother and resuming her interrupted life—until she was imprisoned again in August, for four months—but in preparing the more important book, her memoirs, for publication.

There is no way of knowing whether a copy-editor did look over the text of Les *Microbes humains* before it was given to the type-setter, but if there was one, he did a terrible job. Little or no attempt is made in the printed text to unify the spelling of the names of characters, places and esoteric terms, whose variation strongly suggests that initial copyist could not read the handwriting from which he or she was working, and was prepared to make different guesses more or less at random. Nor could the copyist make much sense of the punctuation, and failed utterly to sort it out adequately. The result of those failures, combined with the effects of the circumstances in which the author produced her original manuscript, is that the Dentu text is an unholy mess.

Louise Michel was probably responsible for some of the errors in rendering names and esoteric terms—she was, after all working purely from memory, presumably reproducing numerous words that she had heard spoken but never seen written down, and the punctuation of her original manuscript was probably slapdash. That is excusable; the fact that her lapses not only went uncorrected, but that dozens of others that could not have been her fault were introduced, is less so. Her apparent lack of involvement in the preparation of the publication, beyond the provision of a brief foreword—the book could have benefited from some supervision on her part, if not an entire second draft—is unfortunate, especially in view of the fact that some sections of the text were almost certainly written with the idea in mind that they would later be revised, but never were. In particular, there are several places where text appears to be missing, including one entire chapter, whose pages were presumably lost somewhere along the line. The occasional incoherency of the text is further compounded by the fact that the storyline was apparently steered in such a way as to encompass and take aboard some sections of text that must have been written earlier, and are rather poorly accommodated to the principal plot-line.

Although the text must have been written with publication at least vaguely in mind, the way the story is put together suggests that was not originally intended to be published in its present form. Many passages are synoptic, bearing some resemblance to the skeletal texts that Auguste Maquet used to provide to be fleshed out and embellished by Alexandre Dumas, and it seems highly likely that the narrative was, at one time, intended to be fleshed out and tidied up at a later date. The story is clearly modeled on the classic feuilleton serials of the 1840s, especially those of Eugène Sue and most especially of all *Les Mystères de Paris*, and it certainly contains sufficient incident to make up a text of 250,000 words rather than a meager 60,000. If that was the author's original intention, however, she abandoned the idea, and by the time of its publication, or shortly thereafter, she had formed a different one.

In the different plan, *Les Microbes humains* was to be the first book in a six-novel series. Several periodicals, including *The Nation* and *The Critic* reported in 1887 that the titles of the other five would be *Le Monde nouveau*,[1] *La Débâcle, ou le Cauchemar de la vie* [The Debacle; or, The Nightmare of Life], *Première Étape* [First Stage], *L'Épopée, ou la légende nouvelle* [The Epic; or, The New Legend] and *D'Astre en astre* [From Star to Star]. Only the second volume appeared, in 1888. The *Gazette anecdotique* had reported in 1887 that the author was correcting the proofs of all five of the other volumes, but this appears to have been an optimistic mistake, although it does suggest that she did correct the proofs of the second; there is no evidence that any of the remaining four were every written—which is a pity, given that the schema seems to have embraced not merely a worldwide transformation of the Earth but an expansion of humankind to other worlds, which would indeed have made it an unparalleled epic of anarchist scientific romance.

---

[1] Also available in a Black Coat Press edition as *The New World*, ISBN 978-1-61227-117-0.

Why the project was aborted is unclear; perhaps the initial surge of enthusiasm simply ran out, or perhaps the potential publisher became hostile to the idea (although some contemporary sources suggest that *Les Microbes humains* was a success, there is no hard evidence of the fact, and *Le Monde nouveau* certainly did not sell well). At any rate, the fact that an attempt was made to assassinate her in 1888—she was shot in the head—certainly did not help, nor did the fact that she was subsequently imprisoned again, and then fled France to live in London from 1890-1895. She did continue writing through all of this, but as always, had other priorities to juggle. It is worth noting that the second and third volumes of her *Mémoires* also remained unpublished while she was alive, although she had drafted the entire text while in prison, either because she was never able to get around to preparing it or because that too ran into problems with its prospective publisher.

Given that context, it is not surprising that *Les Microbes humains* is a problematic text, to the extent that the *Revue Britannique*'s reviewer called it "*le roman le plus incoherent, the plus fou, le plus drôle qui ait jamais paru*" [the most incoherent, craziest and oddest novel that has ever been published]. On the other hand, the hectic surge of the variously multi-stranded plot and its often-cursory manner do have a certain charm of their own, permitting the narrative to attain and maintain a pace and abruptness that would not be seen again until the sophistication of the American comic book in the 1950s. The overall impression is that of Eugène Sue on speed, or Paul Féval on fast-forward. The prose and the plot both have a pulp-fiction crudity, but that kind of prose has a verve of its own, and the plot is deliberately calculated to make the jaw drop. The book was, of course, only published because of Louise Michel's notoriety, and any reader who picked it up would have done so expecting to be shocked, but it is difficult to believe that any other writer of the period could have got away with being quite so shocking. One can imagine some other follower of Eugène Sue writing a human vivisection scene in 1886, and perhaps even getting it into print, but not a human vivisection scene in which the victim is hypnotized in order to be able to report on her agony, let alone one in which she gives birth mid-vivisection.

Similarly, one can imagine a successor of Sue or an admirer of Zola writing and publishing a scene of brutal child rape in 1886, but surely not a scene of necrophiliac child-molestation, especially against a background in which it is taken for granted that avid violent pederasty is rampant in the upper strata of society, and that the invariable practice of the law in those and all other circumstances is to let the guilty go free while mercilessly imprisoning and executing the innocent. Given the nature of her legend and her past, however, what else could be expected of a melodrama by Louise Michel? All standardized nineteenth-century melodramas were virtually compelled to conclude with a nick-of-time rescue, a joyous family reunion, a loving marriage and an abundant inheritance, those being the essential elements of a "happy ending" back then, but who could have expected those eventualities from Louise Michel, even in a plot that carefully provides the raw material for all of them? No one, obviously—and she certainly did not let the expectant members of her audience down.

Were they grateful? Apparently not; a few references to the book's success appear to have been based on empty speculation or mistaken assumption. *Les Microbes humains* was never reprinted in France, by Dentu or anyone else (although a new edition has recently been advertized as imminent), and it is presently an extremely rare book, not yet available on *gallica*. It is, admittedly, not a very good book by purely literary standards, although it would have been a lot better had it been properly copy-edited, but it is a remarkable book nevertheless, and a unique book, at least within its own era.

Writing in prison, of course, Louise Michel could not possibly have avoided comparing herself to the most famous of all French imprisoned writers, the Marquis de Sade—all the more so given that the work of her principal model, Eugène Sue, had often been stigmatized as "sadistic," and that Sade had been a prolific producer of scenes of human vivisection and brutal child-rape. Louise Michel cannot have read the first of the major works that Sade composed in the Bastille, *Les 120 journées de Sodome* (written 1785; tr. as *The 120 Days of Sodom*) because it had not yet been published in any form in 1886, but, even though the book was banned, she might have read the most famous work he drafted there, *Justine, ou les malheurs de la vertu* (first written 1787; revised and expanded 1791; tr. as *Justine; or, The Misfortunes of Virtue*). She would have known, of course, that Sade, as an aristocrat in the days of the *ancien régime*, must have enjoyed far more comfortable circumstances in prison than she had to endure, but even so, she must have felt a certain sympathy for him, and probably understood the real import of her forerunner's revolutionary rhetoric far better than most of the people who bandied the word "sadism" around ever did. If Sue's work was "sadistic," than Michel's work is too, augmented by an extra order of magnitude; it mounts a far more savage assault on the misfortunes of virtue than anyone since Sade, but the import of her rhetoric is

11

much more obvious, simply because she was a woman, and thus automatically to be ranged with the victims rather than the ogres. No one could ever think, for an instant, that in reporting the horrors of the human treatment of human beings Louise Michel was approving of them, and she must have felt, rightly, that she was thus at liberty to paint her horrors more broadly and more luridly than anyone else had previously done outside the realms of proscribed pornography, albeit with a certain modesty of terminology and a defiant lack of eroticism.

Louise Michel was born in 1830 at the Château de Vroncourt in the Haut-Marne, where her mother was a servant, fathered either by the châtelain or his scion. She was brought up there by the châtelain's family, to whom she was invited to refer as her "grandparents," and given a good liberal education, in the course of which she took considerable delight in the works of Jean-Jacques Rousseau and Voltaire; she was later able to support her convinced atheism by becoming a devout admirer of Charles Darwin. As a bastard and, in terms of social class, a "half-breed," she was well-primed for hostility to the prevailing social order, and even for a certain resentful truculence.

In 1852, she obtained a certificate that permitted her to work as a schoolteacher, but could not work in state-approved schools because she refused to recognize Napoléon III as head of state following his *coup d'état* in the previous year. In 1854, she opened a school of her own but it failed, and, in 1856, she went to Paris, where she worked in a boarding-school run by one Madame Voillier. In 1865, she opened a day-school of her own, and made a third attempt in 1868. She also wrote a good deal during this period, including poetry, short stories and legendary tales; she was in regular correspondence with Victor Hugo throughout this period, and was considerably influenced by his ideas, although the rumor that she bore him a child has no evidence to support it—one of a great many allegations that helped build and shape her legend but were almost certainly untrue. She contributed to radical periodicals—which was not at all unusual—but her active involvements in the 1860s were relatively moderate; in 1869 she became the secretary of the Societé démocratique de moralisation, an organization established to assist female workers—effectively, to try to ameliorate the circumstances that forced so many of them into prostitution.

She might have remained an obscure schoolteacher and unsuccessful writer indefinitely, having no apparent ambition to become a legend in her own lifetime, but circumstances changed dramatically in 1870 (the year in which she turned forty), with the outbreak of the Franco-Prussian War, the Siege of Paris and the establishment of the Commune. Her initial involvement in the upheaval was as much patriotic as revolutionary; she did what she could to support the cause of National Defense and to consolidate social order after the Empire's collapse, running a canteen and driving ambulances as well as taking an active role in the Comité de vigilance des citoyens du dix-huitième arrondissement de Paris. As president of that committee she met various people who were later to become important political figures, including George Clemenceau, then Maire of Montmartre, and Théophile Ferré, a member of the National Guard who became one of the prime movers of the Commune, and one of its most aggressive promoters. Ferré was sixteen years her junior, but her *Mémoires* do appear to support the allegation that she became infatuated with him, and that her subsequent actions were at least partly guided by that infatuation.

It is now impossible to separate fact from fiction in trying to determine exactly what part Louise Michel played in the Commune; her memoirs are, understandably, a trifle coy and self-serving, and most of the accusations leveled against her in her subsequent trial were almost certainly trumped-up. It seems probable that all of the most widely-repeated rumors—including the allegation that she volunteered to assassinate Adolphe Thiers, the head of the provisional government that established itself in Versailles in opposition to the Commune, and that she personally set fire to the Hôtel de Ville while wearing a National Guard uniform—were totally fictitious. She did volunteer for the National Guard, and was photographed in its uniform, but her expression and attitude in the picture strongly suggest that she put it on merely in order to be photographed; although she was certainly present at the barricades, attempting to help the wounded, there is no hard evidence that she ever fired a shot, and when she subsequently claimed that neither she nor any other member of the Commune had ever ordered anyone to be shot or set fire to any of the monuments that were burned in the course of the battle for control of Paris, she was probably sincere, if not entirely accurately-informed.

Her legend began to take form when, having escaped after the military suppression of the Commune, she was blackmailed into surrendering by threats made against her mother. Detained with thousands of others at the camp at Satory, she witnessed the summary execution of numerous friends and associates, including Ferré. Like Ferré, she had refused to defend herself at her trial, on the accurate grounds that it was a hollow travesty of justice, and one anecdote more likely to be true than all the rest is that she demanded loudly that her judges sentence her to death. Perhaps, if she had not done that, they would have, but in the event they sentenced her, after two years imprisonment in the Abbaye d'Auberive, to deportation to New Caledonia. By the time of her embarkation in 1871 she had already become famous, assisted by Victor Hugo's campaigning on her behalf and by extensive press coverage, which stuck her with such nicknames as *La Louve rouge* [the Red She-wolf] and *La Bonne Louise*—which, with a slight stretch of the etymological imagination, could be read as "Kindly Louise" rather than "Maidservant Louise" if one cared to do so.

It appears to have been in the course of the four-month voyage to New Caledonia, in company with many other Communards who has escaped the firing-squad, that her political views became refined into the Anarchism in the formulation of whose manifesto she was later to participate, perhaps initially under the influence of the polemicist Henri Rochefort. If the government of the Third Republic had hoped to export her burgeoning legend along with her, however, they failed. She remained a person of interest to the Parisian press, and there was now no longer anything standing in the way of her promotion as a heroine, initially for the assiduity with which she attempted to arrange for the education of the children of the exiles and the children of the native islanders, and then for being (allegedly) the only anarchist among the former Communards to be consistent enough in her views to side with the natives in their rebellion of 1878—the first of many such rebellions. She remained in communication with Hugo, Clemenceau and other supporters in Paris, who campaigned for her release.

Eventually, in 1880, the transported Communards were given a general amnesty, and most of them returned to Paris, including Louise Michel. On arrival she was warmly welcomed by crowds in Dieppe and Paris, and a plaque was eventually erected in Dieppe to commemorate the occasion. She became a popular public speaker and resumed writing; she seemed set for a successful career as a political agitator, but, in March 1883, she took part in a demonstration on behalf of the unemployed, inevitably placed at the head of the march, which ended with a confrontation with the police, and during which three bakers' shops were pillaged. It was for that participation that she was tried in June and received her six-year sentence to solitary confinement —for "incitement to riot"—apparently in an attempt to shut her up for good. Her silence proved, however, to be more eloquent than her speechifying had been, and further campaigns on her behalf eventually forced Grévy to let her out. The four-month sentence she received later that year for making an inflammatory speech in support of striking miners was a great deal wiser in its careful moderation.

The assassination attempt of 1888 came far closer to success in silencing her than any term of imprisonment could have done, although had it succeeded, her martyrdom would probably have been even more eloquent than her enforced silence. When she was imprisoned yet again in 1890, for making another subversive speech, the government attempted to release her almost immediately, but she refused to go unless her fellow prisoners were also released; when she smashed up her cell in protest, the prison doctor wanted to commit her to a lunatic asylum, but the government, by now far more sensitive to potential bad publicity, forbade that. Her subsequent voluntary five-year exile to England was probably far more effective in deflecting attention that any punitive action could have been.

Following her return to Paris in 1895—again welcomed by crowds—she was constantly followed, and repeatedly arrested, by the police; once again, in 1896, she was sentenced to a long term of imprisonment, but Georges Clemenceau was a powerful man by that time, and his intervention soon set her free. She was getting old by then, however, and her political activity gradually tailed off, without ever ceasing, until her eventual death in January 1905. Thousands of people followed her funeral procession, and annual demonstrations took place at her tomb on the anniversary of her death, until the Great War forced their suspension. She remained, and still remains, a key emblem of Anarchist philosophy and agitation, alongside Pyotr Kropotkin, with whom she was associated in both Paris and London. Numerous schools are named after her, and a Metro station.

This translation is taken from the London Library's copy of *Les Microbes humains* (whose date-stamp sheet reveals that it was last taken out in 1975 and contains no record of any loan previous to that date). The translation posed acute difficulties, not merely in the attempt to repair numerous errors of spelling, punctuation and garbled text, but also in the attempted translation of the extensive colorful *argot* employed by some of the Parisian characters, some of which might also have been misrendered by the typesetter (most of it is untraceable in on-line dictionaries of argot). I have attempted to substitute English and American terms of similar import where it is possible to identify or deduce the import, although some inevitably look odd, out of place and anachronistic, but I have made only minimal attempts to suggest the tortured eye-dialect that the original text employs to represent Alsatian waitresses speaking bad French with a German accent. As noted above, I have doubtless made mistakes in trying to winkle out the intended meaning of the more gnomic passages, but I have done the best I could in awkward circumstances, and have footnoted some of the more problematic decisions by way of explanation.

Brian Stableford

THE HUMAN MICROBES

Foreword

This is merely a glance cast over the human microbes swarming in the corruption of our *fin de siècle*.

Through the torments, the old society is about to give birth to a new era; catastrophes are fated to arrive in the crises whose periods are indicated by the break-up of the social organism. Individuals are subjected to their consequences, each of them tending to become responsible at that virile moment of humankind.

Driven to collide with one another like grains of sand in a tidal wave, not yet belonging to the era in which free humans will be truly responsible, we look forward according to the range and accuracy of our vision.

Certain facts cannot be denied. We shall see the disappearance—more veritably annihilated than the savage races disappearing by virtue of the weapons and actions of Europeans—of races weighed down by idleness and numbed by enjoyments, while poverty lashes the blood from the meager flanks of eternally starving races.

Long teeth and avid intelligence are rising everywhere.

Science, scarcely delivered from mythological tongues, is preparing the banquet of a richer life for the human race, the product of greater knowledge.

From the new senses burgeoning at the end of this centuries-old winter, the human sap is rising for the imminent spring, and everything is astir above the rumbling crater.

Nests of vipers are hissing and writhing; hungry wolves are prowling; lions are awakening, raising the hackles of their manes in the uncertain dawn; we are already in the new epic, and the last of the great bards will barely have gone to sleep before the immense choir of bardic legions will be singing the nascent legend over the entire Earth.

It the drama has escaped the excessively narrow theaters, that is because it is already in the street.

If there is no longer a great solitary poet, it is because poetry is blowing on the four winds of heaven over the breathless crowds.

Harmony is awakening for all of us. Wagner anticipated it in his enormous choirs.

Soon will come sequences of notes as intimate as the breath of the wind, and others, on a larger scale; and when, after glissandos that will no longer be audible to our ears, they cover larger distances, that will be an enormous source of musical richness. We have experienced it down here when, after the quarter-tones sounded by the cyclone to the Canaques in one of our distant colonies,[2] a frisson caused the nerves to quiver as if they were the strings of a harp.

The arts are for everyone; neither the eye, nor the voice, nor the ear ought to be useless, and it is bad for us to be incomplete. When every human being is fully-developed in all the senses, and in new senses, it is un-

---

[2] The "Canaques," or Kanaks, in question are the natives of New Caledonia, whose revolt against French colonial rule Michel had supported.

deniable that humankind entire will have a degree of development that we cannot comprehend.

In the meantime, the sky is dark, misery is great, and the new senses are burgeoning in such a hostile environment that they sometimes become monstrosities.

Of those who dread the unknown, some deny the light of tomorrow, others want to know exactly what that light will display—as if one were to demand that the blind protozoa of subterranean lakes take account of the daylight that their descendants, hurled out of the caverns by cataclysms, will see; or as if one had demanded of the inventors of the steam engine what would spring therefrom.

This book, coldly written, is a sketch of the passions of our epoch. At close range, we are dissimilar beings; view from several centuries away, we will resemble ants in the same hive; who can tell whether, for the elevated humankind that will succeed us, any more of our era will survive than the Stone Age has bequeathed to us?

Under borrowed names, real characters are hidden; in the midst of events less romantic than those through which we pass in silence, no one can deny that we are close to the anguish of a transformation.

Everything tends toward the same goal, idioms born from the depths of time, bestial cries, after having invaded the land, like rivers flowing to the same ocean; dialects are fading away into principal languages; soon, perhaps, those languages will be absorbed themselves into that of humankind.

I. By Pipe-Smoke

It is the twenty-sixth of October 18**. The Brasserie du Bel Escholier in the Latin Quarter is overflowing with women.

What do you expect the women to do? The brasserie is the only place where anything is moving! Everywhere else, they can't live, even alone—all the more so when they want to feed some brat half-dead of sloth and paternal excess, whose mother doesn't want to drown it like one kitten too many in the litter.

Those mothers who can't give their children the nourishment of doves, but don't want them to be food from crows, have to enable them to live! It's crueler than killing them, but they hope that they'll be happy. Have you ever seen, when a bird's-nest falls out of a tree, how the female tries to save her brood? It's the same with human nests fallen from the tree of poverty. At the brasserie, in the midst of pipe-smoke and tankards of beer, the girls drink in order to make the clients drink. They have to do their job.

It's a grey evening at the end of autumn, no longer warm enough to sleep under bridges or in the ditches of the fortifications; vagabonds are creeping around, searching with their eyes, beneath lowered pupils, sniffing the air, in search of shelter.

If one listened to what they are saying, perhaps it would be this: "There are so many buildings doing nothing, in which one might take refuge for a while." Workers aren't always obliging—isn't the boss behind them? No sooner do they find someone installed than they get more annoyed than foreman, because they might find themselves on the street like the comrades; they could lose their jobs if they tolerated it.

The poor, having nothing but rags to protect them from the cold, creep around and huddle together like birds, leaving their nests before dawn to resume their eternal peregrinations. Sometimes, they have incredible luck; one day, an old man found some wood-chips, as soft as wool, under a lean-to; it's true that he only got that lucky once; he was so tired that he died there. The rats that were eating him when the odor gave him away never told whether or not they had started while he was still alive. He was so weak that he could scarcely defend himself; the autopsy revealed that he had died of hunger, his stomach as hollow as a lantern.

We shan't get carried away; we'll see worse things in the course of the story, and they're far from equaling the ones we pass over in silence.

At the brasserie, the smoke is so thick that Jupiter could hide behind the cloud.

A bunch of toffs, the verdigrised scrapings of faded root-stocks, are stewing in the hottest corner of the establishment. On a table at the back, they're talking literature; three or four shiverers rummaging through the new works; there are others they don't recognize, "irregulars," they say—those little clowns have infallible futures. One of them unfolds a copy of a student newspaper, the *Totor*, with great precision, and if that doesn't shout out: "I'm a writer!" it's not his fault. He's the one who holds the dice of the conversation; he's recounting how someone named X***, whom neither he nor any of the others likes, has sent him a volume of verse. Yes, X*** has rendered him that homage.

In the middle of the table, another, a little less chilly, listens while smoking; he's enveloped in black smoke, through which he peers occasionally while removing his pipe from his lips.

"That's how it is!" continues the penman. "X*** has dared to send me his book of verse—as if anyone wrote verse nowadays! Oo la la! What a guitar! I read three or four of the little jokes—he's an idiot! Oo la la!"

"What's the title?"

"How do I know? X*** didn't dare put his name on it, but I could tell that it's him. It's enough to make you sleep for twenty-four hours. Oo la la!"

"Are you going to write a review?" asks another shiverer.

"As if! I'm not one to help newcomers and unknowns. There are enough of them, and pretentious with it. The no-name writes eclogues. He wants, he says, to sing like Racan[3] of shepherds and woods. Imbecile!"

"What?" says the least stupid of the wrecks, setting down his pipe—the quotation has touched him sharply, as has the insult, the book attributed to X*** being his.

Have no fear that they'll fight. They won't even bite one another; they're only viper-mimics. They'll only hiss a little; their venom's only drool.

One of the waitresses, a tall brunette with dark-circled eyes often looks sideways, quivering, at a scarcely correct group of young men—who have "had a drink," I guarantee—howling, that being the appropriate term for a conversation in a passionate tone, all of whose participants are "half seas over."

Opposite, two gentlemen, properly dressed with proper manners—too proper, even—are gravely seated, distinguished by all kinds of excessively-visible sobrie-

---

[3] Honorat de Bueil Racan (1589-1670), author of the pastoral drama *Bergeries*.

ty. They aren't smoking, scarcely drinking—expensive wine, it's true—and chatting in moderation.

In spite of this concordance of sobriety, there isn't the slightest rapport between them; they're acting in the same play, that's all; one of them is playing more stupidly than the other, of course. One could as easily credit the one with the upper hand with sixty years as forty; there's nothing living in his face but his eyes, two round eyes, as magnetic as a night-bird's, as cruel as a raptor's. Those eyes efface all the rest; one sees nothing but them, and one would be scared if, instead of being correctly dressed, the gentleman was wearing a vagabond's rags.

The other is a product of modern fattening, but he's the kind of man who eats others' cutlets instead of offering them his. He has the small head and enormous body of an ox of old Albion. Wrapped up in his clothes one might take him for a fat scarab wedged into its wing-cases.

When they came in, the brasserie's little dog hid under a bench, sticking out its head to howl, but the officer charged with surveillance judged that the animal was causing a disturbance and made it understand, with a swift kick, that such manifestations are forbidden. Bristling like a wild boar, it retreated under the bench.

These details were not lost on the incorrectly-dressed group, some noisy, the others silent, who are supping tankards of beer opposite the overly correct men.

One of the silent ones has sketched the neighboring group; he's a thin, dark Irishman—the other is a young madman, a reporter for a subversive newspaper, who has illustrated his scribble, following the Irishman's example, with the same two faces, which would have pleased an artist.

The brunette, who, while going back and forth across the brasserie, finds the means to stimulate drinking by chatting instead of having a drink—which spares her the torture of drinking in spite of having had enough—often looks at the Irish artist. She has a certain wit and dispenses it freely, which keeps the imbeciles at a distance.

The clients like to chat with the beautiful young woman, as bold as a man and as reserved as a little girl. This evening, she's distracted by the sight of the Irishman; her verve is less marked than usual; there's a mist of melancholy over her wit.

At the artist's table, laughing wholeheartedly, are two young men closely resembling one another, long-legged, alert and hot-blooded, with brilliant eyes; one is a creole, the other originally from Marseilles; the memory of the sea haunts their dreams, but they have no time to pause for reverie; they're gaily taking the road to rude combat.

Julius Borelli, the creole, writes combative literature; in the hands of some, the pen is mightier than the sword, and he wants to be one of them.

The other, Pierre Mayard, is a teacher in a day-school; he too tries to fight with his face covered; he's a scholar grafted on to the root-stock of a poet, but he hides that particularity carefully, because people would mock him—as if he had chosen his birth!—and that would be a waste of time.

Julius, who is scribbling his daily bread-and-butter, does not lose sight either of the dog or the two correct gentlemen; he makes portraits of them in a style as realistic as possible; the animal resemblances of the two men are unspared, and obtain the agreement of the Irishman, whose eyes approve. He fixes the two faces at the top of the piece of paper, emerging like a figurehead from the mouth of the dog, drawn below.

No detail has escaped Julius; he has heard the plaint of the anguished beast; that has sent a shiver down his spine and he gazes as the little animal with the bristling hair when it sticks its head out from time to time.

One of the gentleman, the one who resembles a dung-beetle—that being what Julius understands by "scarab"—is reading a news item in a low voice, which he punctuates with his reflections. The other, the man with the round eyes, replies briefly to the reflections of the reader who is attempting to pontificate about the news item.

"Human remains found in the Bièvre have been sent to the morgue. The remains were a femur and a sawn-off piece of skull. They were fished out near the Poplars, where the Bièvre enters Paris; they must have come from the Clamart amphitheater.[4]

"What good does it do," the scarab adds, "to re-count these things in public? It only stirs up trouble." So saying, he nods his head, as if something has fallen on his scalp and he is trying to get rid of it.

The other is not pontificating, and says in an acid tone: "My dear Monsieur, the public loves that! If there were no crimes, there are people who wouldn't sleep tranquil; people like horror, in order to be able to tremble in security."

"What about morality?" the scarab goes on. "My opinion is that crime novels ought to be banned; they put ideas in criminals' heads."

---

[4] Clamart was one of the ancient cemeteries of Paris; in 1884 a dissecting-theater was built there for the purposes of anatomical research.

The man with the round eyes smiles. "My dear Monsieur," he says, emphasizing the syllables with his acrid voice, "when novelists think up such things, it's because they're feverish; they only talk about exaggerated things; anyway, they never know such things as they are, unless they're in the business, and then it would be stupid slander."

Well, well! The correct gentlemen is philosophizing as if he were "in the business" himself. And Julius, obsessed with that thought, studies the gentlemen even more closely. The latter, sensing the gaze, fixes his round eyes on the young man.

Two of the brasserie waitresses are chatting, half in French and half in German, while playing—these without distraction—their role as cup-bearers; they're almost drunk, but are still drinking anyway, to engage the clients. Both blondes, with black-ribbon butterflies on their heads, they're daughters of Alsace, with the slightly pudgy faces of beer-drinkers.

"Always trinking gives one a tick head, eh, Fraouchen?"

"It's the lousy beer in tis place, my tear Rosen."

"I neat to get out!"

"Me too, but you're skint; tose with flannelette knickers can decamp, not us."

(The fault is not with their argot but with their French.)

"My tear Rosen, it upsets the stumach to hit the bottle without a tirst."

(That what they hate the most, in fact; the brasserie waitresses obliged to drink feel sea-sick.)

"Me, I'm always thirsty without being able to hit the bottle," exclaims the café-concert singer, laughing as she downs a glass of absinthe to refresh her throat."

"Shut up!" says one of the girls, sobered by fear. "You'll get me the sack—they'll think I'm complaining and kick me out."

"And she'll get your job." (Frauchen has disappeared.)

"Oh, she promised me she wouldn't! What if she's gone to tell the boss..."

"Hey—Rosen's playing her tune again!" says a fat black waitress with the look of an ant. "You need to drink to get maggots in your belly. Me, I think it's good to get drunk. That's what empties us of melancholy, isn't it? The cramps go away in time. Here, my darling, knock it back—I'm pouring."

She brings another glass of absinthe for the singer.

At the other end of the room, a group of pimps are eyeing up a girl who was formerly the mistress of a guillotine-victim—such celebrities are much sought-after. Old artillerymen have offered to marry her, but they only had the guns—she wants the guns loaded, for choice; she'd be very stupid, wouldn't she, to let herself get rolled over? It's for her that her cavalier snuffed an old lady; she knew his worth—it was her who turned him in, and claimed the reward.

She also knows the price she demands for parading in the brasseries. There she attracts a crowd of imbeciles in quest of perverted sensations; they love the odor of a Charlot basket.[5]

It seems that at the table of the ill-dressed, they're waiting to meet someone—for nothing very serious, but

---

[5] "Charlot"—a diminutive of Charles—is nowadays most familiar in France with reference to Charlie Chaplin, but in 1886 its unqualified use still conjured up the phantom of Charles Sanson, the executioner of Loluis XVI and Marie Antoinette.

still, it's a rendezvous—but then again, realists go to the Brasserie du Bel Escholier to see the group surrounding the mistress of the guillotine-victim. It's worth the trouble!

One of the drunks has a skull like a kneecap, horribly flat, and the mouth of a pike; another, little blinking eyes beneath short rigid lashes. We'll say politely that he has the face of a boar; perhaps he's descended—without any wordplay—from the wild boar of the Ardennes.[6] That's a great feudal name. Here's another representative of the nobility, small and thin with avid red eyes; almost a dwarf, only his eyes and mouth are large. This monster looks like an octopus; his hands are hairy; he reproduces the ancestral type of a remote ancestor omitted from the genealogy of his family. An enormous financier takes up enough room for six; one might think he's a mastodon; he's totally round, and his face has no more expression than the head of a leech; his feet seem to be in a sack one only sees the mouth and the enormous jaws.

And so many others, so many others!

The fat black girl and the octopus are talking in low voices, doubtless about something that resembles them.

It's this group the Irishman sketches, while Julius scribbles and the others chat and smoke.

Still at the same table, here's a drama critic. He has a box for the new play at the Palais-Royal (*Madame Pouffart*) and has come to look for a couple of friends; it won't cost him anything—which is within everyone's means—and besides, it's a comedy, and the grotesque

---

[6] A famous animal of prodigious size, much hunted and finally killed, in 1485, which lived on in legend and literature.

always gives rise to black ideas. It's inspiring for the drama, and makes it all the more pleasant for the author.

Julius and Pierre Mayard accept. The Irishman, for his part, has noticed the girl with the black eyes and goes over to her.

"I don't believe," he says, "that you have anything in common with anyone I've known, but it's necessary that I talk to you."

Both tremble as they arrange a rendezvous for the following morning, not daring to ask for more.

This rendezvous surprises the young men; the Irishman isn't one for arranging rendezvous. That devil Odream. Who would have believed it?

But they see so many things that, a few moments afterwards, they're no longer thinking about it.

Two more young men arrive, semi-bourgeois students this time, who'll get bogged down in the sandbank. They still have clear heads. They chat; they debate; they argue; they lose their heads; they gesticulate—with the result that a carafe falls on the tankards and knocks them over; everything that can fall over follows suit; liquids pour out. They jump back. There go the chairs. Julius' papers fall off; he picks them up, shaking off the water that covers them, not wanting to lose the two caricatures at the head of his article.

The correctly-dressed man has seen the faces. He looks with his round eyes at Julius, who looks back at him. They certainly won't forget one another.

The fall of the chairs attracts the establishment's waiters, and the officer, who wants to throw out the noisy group, who drink so little but break things so noisily, but a new arrival reestablishes calm. He's a Russian who sports the legendary name of Olaff. Tall, with dark blue eyes, hair as bushy as a mane and the broad and bulbous forehead of a bear, one scarcely ever sees him with the same expression; from one moment to the next, his mobile face follows his thoughts.

Comrade Olaff, as his friends call him, is looking for them to say goodbye. He's going away for a few months, and is on his way to the railway station. Olaff pays for the breakages—he's in funds for the moment—and the ill-dressed band takes its place at a tidier table, having ordered more beers in order to stay.

During the uproar, Julius has seen that the little dog, now free, has sneaked up on the man with the round eyes and ripped the bottom of his trousers, perhaps nipping his ankles slightly; the man, not wanting anyone to find out about the dog's sentiments, has contented himself with crushing its paw beneath his foot. All that has happened silently; Azor, understanding that he ought not get so close to his enemy's legs, has gone back into hiding.

The officer no longer remembers that he had sent someone to fetch reinforcements when the agents arrive. A stormy explanation ensues, and further uproar, even noisier. Olaff forms a bulwark for Julius, who is finishing off his article for the subversive paper for which he writes about communal misery.

He has a fist of iron, that Olaff, but here come more agents; the young men can't hold out. The Irishman, an inoffensive spectator thus far, having hastily sketched the scene, with his paper against the wall, comes to the rescue, using the flat of his hand like an Irish dagger, driving the assailants back by striking them in the neck like a butcher. The hand doesn't cut, but it shoves people aside forcefully.

Julius has finished his article, and puts it in his pocket.

Olaff, wanting to get the ridiculous skirmish over and done with, snuffs out the gas-jet burning over the table. A few young men, and even a few of the brasserie girls in places that aren't in view, throw themselves at the jets; the gas goes out and only the street-lights sent a feeble light through the windows.

Followed by the agents, who are groping their way through the tables and knocking them over, the young men hurl themselves outside and disperse in all directions. A few of them go to meet up with their friends in front of the Odéon. There are six of them! No one's missing.

"Are you coming to the Palais-Royal? Are you coming here? Are you coming there?" ask four voices at the same time of the blond with the Herculean fist.

"You know full well that I'm going to the Gare de Lyon."

"That's true—we'll go with you."

"Thanks, but you'll make too much noise for the comrade who's waiting for me there."

"Go, then, you old bear! One might think you were in trouble with the law!"

They shake hands, laughing, and send the bear on his way, calm and confident, toward the station.

The Irishman has gone back to his lodgings, in great haste to be alone.

Julius, Pierre and the theater critic head for the Palais-Royal.

Under the lantern of a tobacconist's shop, Julius takes two preaddressed envelopes out of his wallet—making a mistake, of course, in putting his two missives into them—throws the one bearing the address of his paper into the letter-box, but accidentally drops the other one outside the letter-box. He feels relieved; he has nothing further to do today.

Julius has no suspicion that he has just cast the dice of his fate. He stands there, stunned; the two men occupying his thoughts are in front of him, coming in the opposite direction: the scarab and the man with the round eyes. Have you ever noticed how more frequently you encounter people you aren't expecting than people you are?

While Julius and his friends continue on their way, the man with the round eyes bends down to pick up a little white rectangle standing out against the sidewalk—Julius's letter—puts it in his pocket and continues on his way, in company with the scarab.

What had happened at the brasserie after the departure of the young men was inevitable. As soon as order was reestablished—which is to say, the gaslight was restored—the two gentlemen had left, still correct and grave, even though a further incident had occurred, the latter without Julius noticing it.

While the lights were out, the man with the round eyes had poured into his companion's glass the contents of a minuscule phial concealed in his hand, and had also sprinkled some on a little cake, which he had thrown under the table, intended for Azor (he was not a man to forget anyone). That was imprudent, for the dog was suspicious of the treat, which stank of an enemy hand, and it remained on the ground.

It was not the man with the round eyes who would have to suffer the consequences of that.

Let's return to the Palais-Royal. Julius and his companions were greatly astonished to discover, in the box opposite theirs, still perfectly irreproachable in their appearance, the two correct gentlemen, one still leading the other. Obviously, he didn't know about the business regarding the Bièvre, but Julius was anxious. It was not that he liked the scarab, but he sensed that he was in danger; it was the same sentiment one feels for a drowning dog.

The man with the round eyes calmly unsealed the letter he had found, and read it at his ease.

It appears, Julius thought, *that the gentleman doesn't like to read his letters in front of inconvenient witnesses—there's some story of a woman in that missive he's contemplating.*

Poor Julius!

The round eyes fixed on his article were gazing at it attentively, with good reason.

Under the title *Profiles*, Julius told the story of the incident with the brasserie dog, under grotesque names, with the accompaniment of conjectures that were scarcely flattering. The article concluded as follows:

Whether that bird of ill-omen is seeking live or dead prey, whether he is lying in ambush on his own account or serving as a falcon for others, what is certain is that he's an evil bird.

That animal has evil designs. Watch out, old chap, that I don't find you at work! You were too scared of letting Azor's sentiments be known not to be a bad lot. And you, Azor, thanks, my boy—but be careful he doesn't throw you in the water, claiming that he's executing a rabid dog.

JULIUS BORELLI

The man with the round eyes put the letter back in his pocket, addressing a vulpine smile to his good luck.

"What the Devil's distracting you, Julius?" said the critic. "One might think that you weren't listening to the play—it's funnier than most comedies, not tiresome at all."

Julius was, indeed, not listening, for a human life in danger is something else; his scarab seemed to him to be in sinister company; he was watching. At a play however, in a crowd, that was impossible.

In order to chase away the thought that was obsessing him, Julius became the most cheerful of the three; after all, the stout man could not be in any danger; he was the other's friend. Nevertheless, the thought kept coming back. He became sad while the entire audience laughed like crazy.

As for the scarab, he laughed enough to make his fat belly quiver beneath his wing-cases. He even laughed so long and hard that he suddenly collapsed.

He was carried out and lavished with care; a physician immediately came to his aid, but it was all in vain—for those who noticed it.

That death cast a chill over the remainder of the performance.

Julius had nothing but probabilities; he had not even sufficient grounds to be able to warn the victim—who would not have believed him anyway. However, his heart swelled as if he had been able to prevent the catastrophe, so simple that no one would have believed him.

Aren't sudden deaths frequent? The newspapers recorded them every day. Perhaps it was only that. Was he going mad?

But what about Azor?

Bah! Dogs aren't infallible.

As he was about to go back into his lodgings, Julius saw a light in the window of the Irishman Odream, whom we met at the brasserie. Odream lived above Julius. He had the idea of confiding his anxieties to him.

"I agree," said the Irishman, "that bizarre things often happen, but you can't bring your scarab back to life, can you? Nor can you denounce the other on the grounds that he looks like a bird of ill-omen and that a dog bit him."

"For a start, I never denounce anyone."

"If you did it in these circumstances, with Azor as your only witness, they'd put you in the hands of an alienist, and they wouldn't be wrong."

"You can't deny that it's strange, though."

"I don't deny it."

"What can I do, then?"

"Absolutely nothing. The man can't be resurrected; it's necessary to consider it as a *fait accompli*."

"There's scarcely any way to consider it otherwise."

"That's true. There are fatalities."

"You ought to know about strange things. For one thing, you're not called Odream. It's a pseudonym, wordplay to signify that you come from a land of dreams."

"On the contrary; I come from a place where people no longer dream."

"What do you mean?"

"This morning, I wouldn't have wanted to tell you this; now, it's different. You need to talk too; it'll do you good, and I know you're discreet. No, my name isn't Odream; I adopted that name after I was hanged."

"Hanged? Now you're not making sense."

"Certainly, hanged—but the thing was done summarily, by drunken soldiers, while sacking a region. They were short of rope and came back to get mine, thinking I was dead. I wasn't, that's all—it's quite simple. It was in Ireland, during the last insurrection; they hanged six of us, like a chandelier, from the branches of the willows by the roadside. When they took me down to get the rope they threw me in the grass. The night dew brought me round, it seems. I was young and strong; I remember it as if it were today. It was in spring; there were roses in the grass in Ireland; one might have taken them for huge drops of blood. I got up, tottering, and went back to my house; it had been burned; my wife and daughter had disappeared."

"Your wife! Your daughter? How long ago was this, and how old are you?"

"Thirty! We grow old slowly; the Irish race stays green for a long time, and even if it's cut down like a hayfield, it always grows back tall and sturdy."

"Are you sure that your wife and daughter are dead?"

"I've been looking for them for ten years, on the basis of presumptions as poorly founded as yours regarding the man with the round eyes. I always will, guided by some instinct that says to me: *you'll see them again*—and at the same time. I recognize the impossibility of searching thus for two stems in a scythed crop. Nevertheless, I go on. I've traveled across Europe, and thanks to my talent in drawing, which permits me to blend in anywhere, I've followed, as one follows a mirage, the legend of the hanged man's diamonds, which made my daughter such a rich heiress, for which many claimants for her dowry are searching at the same time as me. You can compare my persistence to that of Lady Franklin having the polar ice explored."[7]

---

[7] Sir John Franklin led an expedition to find the North-West Passage in 1845 and never came back; aided by the American

"Aren't you being irrational, with your hanged man's diamonds?"

"Less than you were just now with your man with round eyes. The diamonds exist, I put them in a safe place myself—alas!—for my beloveds, who will never come back."

"And you haven't sold them to help in your search?"

"Only one—the least valuable; the others are waiting for my daughter and her mother."

"Olaff would tell you that they could support a people in revolt."

"Olaff has a revolutionary passion; my passion is for my vanished darlings."

"And you've never found a single clue?"

"Once there was more than a clue; I saw a young woman with a perfect resemblance to Georges—Georges is my wife—but aged twenty years in ten. Perhaps it wasn't her, but who knows? They had to leave without resources, and it was necessary to bring up her daughter."

"When did you see her?"

This evening, at the brasserie—but no, it wasn't her. And yet, that woman had a glint in her eyes, and the impossible sometimes happens."

"Are you going to see her again?"

"We're meeting this morning—which is to say, five hours from now; it's two o'clock."

---

newspapers, his wife (or rather, his widow) made such a fuss that several more expeditions were sent, in succession to find him. More men perished looking for him than had been in the original expedition.

"Oh, that's what it was!" said Julius. "We thought you'd got lucky."

The Irishman laughed sadly.

They parted at dawn.

Instead of going to bed, Julius went to work; he occupied himself with a host of things, especially the sciences; he brought home enough chemical products to terrify the whole world.

The thought of the man with the round eyes came back to haunt him, though; he thought about crimes that went unsolved because those who had committed them were reputedly honest, about human stupidity, and the prejudices beneath which those vipers sheltered eternally, and poor Julius felt sad.

What he was waiting for, curled up in an old armchair, it would have been impossible for him to say. Perhaps one scents events coming, having inherited an ability from our bestial ancestors, which scented the approach of an enemy.

The readers of the subversive paper for which Julius wrote were very surprised when they eventually read the following, inserted in confidence, under the usual rubric of *Profiles*:

My old bear,

I'll send this to Lyon, since you're going to spend a week there.

I don't believe that it will be possible for you to come back, so write immediately to the friend of whom you've often spoken to me, and ask him to obtain a second witness unknown to our entourage.

It concerns my sister; I want the matter to remain secret; I'm writing to you, being unable to see you alone this evening.

No one must know anything about this affair. Some mud always sticks to a woman for whom one fights a duel.

Our mutual friends are as ignorant as anyone else as to the reasons for the duel, which are that my sister has been grossly insulted by a filthy pig by the name of Sylvain Mirbel; you will understand that I want to kill the rotten beast without having all the trumpets of the press before me, and that, in the contrary case, the true reason for the duel must not become known.

I'm counting on you; hurry.

Goodbye, and thanks.

JULIUS BORELLI

The idea of publishing a letter in which one begs secrecy for something that one wants to hide was astonishing at first; then the article was considered as a joke; it was, in any case, so lacking in significance that no one would have paid any attention to it without the name of the fat financier being printed in full; that was defamation.

Julius, unaware of all these things, fell asleep during the day. He woke up abruptly when someone knocked on his door.

Had his friend Olaff sent a telegram already? No, the letter couldn't even have reached Olaff; it wasn't yet midday.

II. Arrests

At the arranged time, Odream knocked on the door of the brunette woman from the Bel Escholier, and it opened wide. A police commissaire, his secretary and four agents were in the room. Standing in front of the commissaire, the woman was being subjected to an interrogation.

A child with an enormous head charged with a forest of red hair, whose face was old and his figure rickety, took advantage of the opportunity to slip through the agents' legs and go down the stairs in the furtive manner of a fleeing rabbit.

"What do you want?" asked the commissaire.

"I want to talk to the lady who lives here."

"What about?"

"My family. I recognized a resemblance between her and one of its members."

The unfortunate woman shivered at the sound of the Irishman's voice. They recognized one another, conclusively. Overcome by emotion, the woman fainted.

"What's your name?" the commissaire asked Odream, while the woman was transported, on his orders, to a fiacre. He had also ordered that "the boy" be taken to the foundling home, but the child was far away, running through Paris, going to the end of one street and then another, threading his way through them like a bootlace, with the instinct of a hunted animal.

The words "the boy" had an impact on Odream; it was not the fact that the commissaire had demanded his name but the order to take "the boy" to the foundling home that made his heart lurch. To whom, then did the boy belong? He had not thought that the child could be anyone but his daughter.

As for his wife, he mind refused to comprehend. "I don't know what crime the lady has been accused of," he said to the commissaire, "but if she's the person I suppose, she hasn't committed any. The child of whom you speak is not a son but a daughter of about eleven. I could have resisted when I was rebuffed just now, but my first priority is to save the accused person. Her name ought to be Georges O'Patrick, and the child's name is Ellen."

The commissaire replied: "The woman we've just arrested is a Spaniard named Luiza Cardenio, and she's accused of complicity in poisoning. She helped extinguish the gas in the Bel Escholier; her son appears to be about six or seven years old. I've just sent him to the foundling home."

The Irishman was trembling so much that the commissaire said to himself: *This one's guilty too.*

"What's your name?"

"O'Patrick; I'm known under the pseudonym Odream. I'm that woman's husband and Ellen's father; such a resemblance can't be a coincidence; they're the cherished individuals I'm looking for, Georges and Ellen."

"Georges is a man's forename—are you serious?"

"She was brought up under that name, in masculine clothing."

"Where? By whom?"

"At the University of Edinburgh, by a scientist who took the place of her father until we were married." He then confessed everything that he knew; that she was the daughter of an Irishwoman who had died in an Edinburgh hospital. "Ellen was following the University courses with us; her sex was discovered; we fell in love and I married her."

The commissaire thought he was dealing with a madman. "When did you adopt the pseudonym Odream?"

"After my execution."

His execution! This time the commissaire was convinced; Odream was mad. *These poor artists!* he said to himself, compassionately, while having the Irishman taken, under careful guard, to a sanitarium, where no one paid any further heed to him for several days.

Odream attempted to explain, but the anxiety in his face, the assertion he had made to the commissaire that he had been hanged, and a thousand insignificant things taken for symptoms of alienation all turned against him.

The next day, the newspapers announced that the caricaturist, having suddenly gone mad, had been interned at   . He was well-known. A band of reporters was dispatched by the joyful newspapers to the sanitarium. It is easy to see a madman in the circumstances in which he found himself.

Odream had not yet been accused of anything and the pen-pushers were allowed to interview him to request. At first he was polite, but then he got angry. When one imbecile, smiling at his every word—catching them on the wing as birds swallow insects—asked him, while taking his tongue between his pursed lips: "Do you remember how you felt when your neck was squeezed?" Odream replied: "You'll find out," seizing the imbecile by the neck with his hands and shaking him like a rag.

Everyone thought that he was going to strangle the joker, who was dragged from his hands without delay. Odream, put back into his straitjacket, was consigned to the section for furious madmen.

Since they're obstinate in believing me mad, he thought, *I prefer ill-treatment to the curiosity of those clowns. It'll be over sooner.*

He was wrong.

III. Julius

On the same day as the arrest of the woman from the café and Odream, Julius awoke at midday, torn from the morning slumber that that overtaken him. Surprised by the knocking and wondering who it could be, he did not have long to consider the question. It was the commissaire—the same one who had made the morning's arrest. He was accompanied by a squad of agents. All the "criminals" had been denounced by an anonymous letter from the man with the round eyes. Evidence had already been accumulated; there's never any lack of it to prove that lanterns are stars.

"Your name is Julius Borelli?"

"Yes; is it about yesterday's brawl?"

"You were born in Senegal?"

"Yes, but that has nothing to do with the brawl."

"Yesterday evening between seven and eight o'clock you were in the Brasserie du Bel Escholier, with several young men whose complicity will be examined. At a table opposite yours there were two perfectly respectable gentlemen."

"Respectable? If you say so."

"You don't have to make your appreciation known; you've proved it in a sinister fashion!"

"My God, Monsieur, my appreciation is that, the broken glasses having been paid for, we were quite tranquil when someone came to annoy us by restoring the order that no one was troubling any longer. Those who committed that aggression deserved the clouts they received; I don't regret therm."

"Cease expressing yourself with that levity, accused; it's not a matter of the brawl but the crime that you committed while your female accomplice and men yet to be arrested were putting out the gas at the end of the fight."

"If you're calling my article a crime, I certainly wrote it while everyone could see clearly—but hang on, that gives me a suspicion. You're no more a commissaire of police than I am; you're a practical joker, and this farce has gone on long enough." He started laughing frankly, showing his teeth, as white as a puppy's.

The strange form of the search carried out under the commissaire's orders, which was principally directed toward ointment pots, chemical products and trinkets, etc.—including a grafting-saw—instead of being directed toward his papers, confirmed the young man in the idea that he was dealing with practical jokers.

He's a clever criminal, the commissaire said to himself.

"Perhaps there's been a mistake," said Julius. "Come on, Monsieur, if you really are a commissaire, of what am I accused? Is it of having stolen the Palais de Justice while the gas was out?"

"You're accused of having poisoned, during that interval, the cakes that were on the next table, of which Monsieur Valfort, landowner of Cyprès, near Marseilles, died yesterday evening at the Théâtre du Palais-Royal."

Julius unleashed an immense burst of laughter, and thus become thoughtful.

"You might have mistaken the address," he said.

"What do you mean?"

"I don't accuse anyone on the basic of suspicions; I'll see by the way things go whether I ought to talk; I can almost believe that you're really going to arrest me, anything's possible—except that evidence is required to keep someone in prison. It has to be proved that I've committed a crime."

"Or you have to prove that you haven't committed one."

That was how Julius was arrested and put in solitary confinement.

IV. Formal Accusation

On the twenty-sixth of October last, between eight and nine p.m., a brawl broke out between the representatives of the public force and a few young men who were disturbing the peace at the Brasserie du Bel Escholier.

The gas having been extinguished at the end of the brawl by them and a brasserie waitress known by the name of Grand-Brune, a person named Julius Borelli, originally from Senegal (the denouncer had known Julius' name by virtue of the signature on the article, and his origin was known) *threw on to the cakes that would have been consumed by Messieurs Valfort, a landowner of Cyprès, in the vicinity of Marseilles, and de Gore, a rentier of Paris, a violent poison, of which Monsieur Valfort died almost immediately. Monsieur de Gore is still ill.*

One of the cakes, found under the table, has been subjected to expert analysis; a poison particular to Senegal was found therein. (This came fatefully to the support of the denunciation, the dog having left the poisoned cake.)

Julius Borelli must have had previous communication with Monsieur de Gore via one of his friends, Monsieur Sylvain Mirbel, the lover of Julius' sister; the latter has disappeared. His recognized honesty leads to the supposition that he too has been a victim. A considerable number of witnesses have seen Messieurs Julius Borelli, de Gore and Mirbel together.

A saw hidden in Borelli's lodgings is perfectly adapted to the section of a skull found in the Bièvre,

close to the Poplars, with a human tibia—bones as-
sumed to belong to the unfortunate Sylvain Mirbel.

A person named Olaff (the man with the round eyes)
had heard the name) *and Julius Borelli's other compan-*
ions are accused of complicity in the murder, having
extinguished the gas to facilitate the perpetration of the
crime; and Luiza Cardenio, waitress at the Brasserie du
Bel Escholier, who helped in extinguishing the gas at the
place where she was sitting, is similarly accused of com-
plicity in the assassination, should also be held at the
disposition of the law.

Also to be summoned to appear:

Edmé X***, managing editor of the Revue réaliste,
which published the letter addressed by Julius Borelli to
an imaginary individual with the goal of leading justice
astray, in which he issue a death-threat against Sylvain
Mirbel in advance of the accusation, feigning the project
of a duel.

Odream, interned in a sanitarium, will be interro-
gated, if possible, as having taken part in the brawl.

Pierre Mayard, Étienne Fauvel and Marius Ra-
meau will have to render an account of the part played
by them in the extinction of the gas during the poisoning
of Monsieur Valfort by Julius Borelli at the Brasserie du
Bel Escholier. (Martin Rameau was the theater critic
what had taken Julius and Pierre Mayard to the Théâtre
du Palais-Royal.)

Justice works swiftly, and is rarely deceived, said
the examining magistrate to himself, considering the accumulated evidence.

Almost all the accused were known to the public
and considered honest; all the arrests were therefore
greeted with amazement. People wondered whether it

might not be a sensational rumor. A few went to Julius' lodgings and those of the other accused. It was true!

The examining magistrates themselves, while admiring the promptitude and reliability of the information, wondered why, in that strange affair, neither the accused nor his accomplices seemed capable of such a crime. (All things considered, it scarcely seemed probable).

Many other items of evidence appeared, brought forward by unknown hands; it seemed that a powerful will was pushing Julius toward La Roquette[8] and the others toward prison.

The judges felt no obligation to worry about where the new evidence came from; they accumulated it, and that was all. No one paid any attention to the man with round eyes. His high status, the honorability of his life, his moderate opinions, the marginal part that he had played in the drama, seemingly distant from Monsieur Valfort's bad acquaintances, such as Julius Borelli—who had just revealed himself, to general amazement, as a great criminal—and the reluctance he had shown in testifying, all gave Monsieur de Gore the role of a sage who had attempted to protect his provincial correspondent while showing him around Paris, and have almost shared his deadly fate.

The justice went to see Monsieur de Gore at home; he was now in bed, after having tried to devote himself to business as usual.

As for Sylvain Mirbel, his fate was too certain for anyone to search for him any longer. He must have per-

---

[8] Two prisons were opened at La Roquette in the 1830s; the guillotine was moved to La Grande Roquette in 1851, where all executions in Paris were carried out thereafter.

ished, a victim of Julius' anger against de Gore, with whom hi sister had compromised herself.

The accused individuals did not see one another until the trial; they had been interrogated separately. Julius' mother and sister had been put in detenticn; he expected to see them together in the dock, but only his sister was there.

"Where's my mother?" he asked her.

"She's ill," the young woman replied, not daring to tell him the frightful truth. Everyone kept quiet about it. Julius' mother had died the previous day. The magistrates' pity thought to ease the end of the first session by waiting to tell him the terrible news.

Julius greeted the audience with his childishly incredulous and innocent laughter; that smile sealed his doom.

"What a bandit!" said those who did not know that the frightful news had been hidden from him.

"What a monster!" they said in the audience. "He laughs when his mother is dead! Perhaps he poisoned her!" The imbeciles forgot that they had not been in the same prison.

The hearing of the witnesses began, beginning with those for the prosecution.

The first was a waiter at the brasserie who, under the influence of Monsieur de Gore, had ended up believing that Julius had brushed past him when the latter must have left his seat to go to the victim's table. A little crystal or glass bottle was in his hand; the waiter had seen it glittering in the dark.

"Accused," said the president, "have you any response to this evidence?"

"I don't respond to follies; the common sense of the public will do them justice."

But public common sense was beginning to follow a false trail, misled as it was by the whispers in the hall. Who had said them first? Does one ever know? They followed their path, impressing the audience.

Someone had said that Julius' father had died a victim of poison. A letter from him, sent to his mother in her prison, had made the poor woman ill, and she had died of that illness; the letter must have been poisoned; perhaps despair had revealed too much.

The piece of cake that had fallen under the table had been offered to the little dog who had started howling; that as why, the morning after the crime, the piece of cake had been taken to a doctor for analysis, and had been found to be poisoned; that fact corroborated the anonymous denunciation.

The fact was true, but Azor's howling had not been addressed to Julius. ("Facts don't lie," it was said.)

A second waiter from the brasseries gave the same testimony as the first.

A third and a fourth had seen Julius slipping through the darkness. They believed it; there are contagions of the mind; what one says that he has seen, others are persuaded that they have seen.

If all of those who have had political trials—and who, in consequence, say frankly what they have done—took the trouble to count up the stupid things that they have not done, but which certain witnesses have seen them do, there would be numerous proofs to support this observation. Some have been heard saying something ridiculous, which merely signifies the deranged mental state of the witness. One of us was able to hear himself accused of having laughed at the door of an old harpy of whose existence he was utterly unaware.

Thus was Julius accused.

As soon as one witness thought he had seen him, the others were sure that they must have seen him too. Is it the desire to do harm that makes people act in this manner? No, it's human stupidity.

A few waitresses were less stupid; they were sure that they had not seen anything.

"Nein, nein," Frauchen had said, at first. "I won't lie." Soon, however, she thought that she had seen something that she could not make out very clearly; the suggestion took hold; Frauchen had seen Julius pass by. Rosen claimed to have seen the same thing, but did not know what it was.

The fat black waitress had seen everything! (A matter of showing off to the tribunal.) She explained that Julius had some from the back of the brasserie to reach the table opposite hers; no one thought about the distance he would have had to travel.

As for Angélique, the mistress of the guillotine-victim, she wanted to pose for the magistrates; she was recognized there; she had already given evidence in the trial of her boy-friend; al the perverts who surrounded her every evening had got front row seats.

The narration of that scene could fill two hundred pages, and there would still be more to say. The male and female witnesses who affirmed that they had seen Sylvain Mirbel, Monsieur Valfort, Julius and his sister together were evidently doing so in good faith; they were nevertheless wrong.

Implausibility came closer and closer to reality.

Julius, whom the president asked whether he had anything to say in his defense, replied: "My God, Monsieur, if you've read Edgar Poe you'll know as well as I do how implausible all this is."

Diana Borelli uttered a cry of indignation when she heard herself accused of having had "relations" with Mirbel—she had only seen him once, on the day when he had insulted her with his propositions. She had not been the mistress of Sylvain Mirbel or anyone else. One day, that individual had mistaken her for a woman he knew; that scarcely flattering resemblance explained the error of certain witnesses; as for her brother, she was equally sure of his innocence.

The young men accused of complicity thought, like Julius, that the trial was fantastic, but took it seriously.

By virtue of listening to the crushing evidence against Julius, they recalled his preoccupation; then they remembered something else: the article Julius had written; but they did not understand how the article had been replaced by the letter. Had he wanted to alert the law? Julius did not understand that substitution himself. If there had been, as Julius thought, a mistake with the envelopes, Olaff would have replied—but no one had heard any word of Olaff.

As for the Irishman, when he was asked whether he still claimed to have been hanged, and had replied in the affirmative, he was not interrogated any further. He did not appear at the trial, being recognized as insane.

The brunette woman, not knowing what Odream had said, and understanding that he was thought to be mad, did not want to complicate the unfortunate man's situation; she kept quiet. What would she have said, anyway? No one had even told her about the crazy things said by the man who claimed to be her husband; having the charge of complicity in murder laid against her, she did not want to drag him into the St. Vitus's Dance that the affair was becoming.

She was condemned, along with Diana Borelli, to five years in prison; the others were acquitted; as for Julius, he was condemned to death.

The man with the round eyes had been clever; he did not appear that the trial; he had told the examining magistrate that he had not seen anything and his health no longer allowed him to be transported. It was all the more skillful on the part of the man with the round eyes that he brought everything about without compromising himself in the slightest. The spider, having woven his web, was able to hide himself safely; everything pointed to the culpability of the accused.

The witnesses for the defense did not come. Julius was still counting on Olaff, but chance was the accomplice of the man with the round eyes. Olaff had not stayed in Lyon, as Julius thought; he had received a telegram from the English ship *Whale,* which was to set sail in two days, and on which he had booked passage. *Whale*, a whaling vessel, was going to the South Pole— which does not seem consonant with the subject preoccupying Olaff, but which was, in reality, connected with it. He was already far away in the southern ocean when Julius was condemned to death.

In order for him to have given his address in Lyon it is probable that the Russian, knowing his friend's character, had the habit of watching over him. He had also charged with that care, at the moment of his departure, the friend of whom Julius had spoken in his strange letter—but when precautions are turned inside out they make a trap.

At the moment of Julius' condemnation, however, there was a frisson in the room—the truth fluttering its wings in passing. That was all.

When the accused were brought back in to hear their sentences, Julius, gripped again by the idea that he was having a bad dream, let out one last burst of childish laughter.

"The wretch!" people murmured, again. "He laughs, and his mother is dead!"

This time, Julius heard them; he uttered a scream, and fainted.

"He's innocent!" cried the clear, strong voice of Diana.

Julius did not want to enter an appeal; his mother's death, added to everything else, was too much, and the conviction that he was not dreaming gradually took hold of him. The idea of ridding himself of the horrible situation by quitting life was not disagreeable to him; he arrived at it at the moment when nothing is any longer redoubtable or desirable; the days followed one another without him thinking about it.

When anyone addressed some gross insult to him, he assumed disdain for the human beast; his heart lurched and that was all.

Fortunately, he thought, *it'll soon be over.*

But death did not arrive.

V. A Story to Put Those Condemned to Death
to Sleep

Six weeks later, at La Grande Roquette, in one of the three condemned cells, Julius was sitting with two agents in front of a set of dominoes, which many cold or enfevered hands had held unthinkingly, their mind far away in the unknown—perhaps dwelling on the probable experiments to which their severed heads would be subjected in the hands of scientists. One thinks about such things when one's days are numbered.

Julius' straitjacket had been removed. Why bother? He would go to the end without seeking death more rapidly; a residue of curiosity made him desire the moment when he would take account of oblivion. Then again, he was not sure that the nightmare would not vanish, that he would not wake up to fond his mother alive and his sister beside him. He had not requested that the straitjacket be removed; the unpleasant sensation that it caused him to experience had aided him in seeking to wake up.

In the midst of that anxious doubt, he wondered exactly where he was bound in strangeness, whether he would be aware of the experiments that were carried out on his cadaver, and whether he would be able to testify by some sign that he could hear the scientists drawing conclusions from those experiments that were contrary to verity. If his brain could take account of them, he would no longer have a voice to say so, his throat being cut, cleanly or otherwise, depending on the skill of the executioner—and he had heard rumor of the awkwardness of those employees of death.

That was what poor Julius was thinking while his guardians strove to distract him.

One of the agents, tall, thin and dark-skinned, was named Jabouille. The other, short in stature, blond and broad-shouldered, named Yvon, appeared to be a Breton.

Why, on seeing the latter, did Julius think of Olaff? He could not have explained it; there are millions of things that magnetism will explain some day, when it will be something other than a key for which some people are searching for the lock and others hiding it with charlatanry.

Jabouille specialized in telling stories; all those condemned to death had been amused by them for two or three years. He was proud of that success.

That evening, from time to time, a murmur came from the Place de la Roquette, like the distant hum of a beehive. Every time that sound arrived, like a gust of wind, Jabouille shuffled the dominoes with which they were not playing, in order to "cheer up the situation." The other did not seem to pay any attention to it.

From beyond the gates of La Roquette, in the noise of the beehive, there were girls singing the songs of the trade they were plying, for the pleasure of gentlemen interested in all the corruptions. There were the voices of men joking coarsely, and the shrill hoarse voices of street-urchins.

That crowd assembled around the human abattoir contained future victims trying to look the blade in the face, criminals come to learn to scorn death, cruel and stupid idlers yawning like wonderstruck carp, and homeless vagabonds taking advantage of the occasion to lie down in a corner against a wall and sleep in peace, their meager rags wrapped around them, making them resemble baby skylarks swaddled in hectic feathers in broad daylight.

Death was bringing that prison-seed to fruition, but they slept peacefully.

There were recidivists there, come to see what would happen to them some day...the pitcher that goes oftenest to the well, etc. There were deranged individuals in quest of "emotions," and even sane individuals aware that the wolf's mouth is the safest shelter. There were scientists preoccupied with the persistence of organic life waiting a little further away, sure of getting good places. For them, there was scarcely any difference between men on the scaffold and beasts in the laboratory gutter. Journalists, lying in ambush for realistic conversations, were slithering wherever they could—there was no shortage of horrible conversation.

"What, are you here, Camuche?"

"Where else would I be? But I won't come any more. The last time left me blasé."

"Oh, me, I've been blasé for a long time. It's not drinking the sea; one only has to hold still for a moment and it's all over. One doesn't die twice; feeling hunger pangs all the time—that can last a lifetime."

"Who did he kill, the comrade they're chopping?"

"No idea—some rich bastard, apparently."

Men in flapped caps prowl around the girls like dogs around a flock; those individuals are pimping out the unfortunates or looking for swollen pockets in order to take the swelling down while the girls amuse the marks with lewd talk.

Around the square there is a cordon of soldiers; others are keeping clear the space in which the scaffold is being built. The paving stones are wet with mud; soon they'll be red with blood, as if an ox had just been slaughtered. The street-urchins will soak their handkerchiefs in it.

The crowd has eddies like the sea, whirlpools and waterspouts, furies and calms; the human waves have their ebb and flow, but this isn't the crowd of epic struggles, which unfurls the flag enflamed by the dawn; it's the crowd that likes to see blood flow. There are people of high and low status who have that taste—people of high status especially.

The square has been well-washed; one can smell a fresh and insipid odor there, like that of a butcher's stall.

When the human buzz is louder, it arrives in gusts in the cell; one might think that it is far, far away!

On those occasions, Jabouille rattles the dominoes desperately.

So Julius understands that the thing is in preparation; a shiver runs down his back. It's not the fear of death; it's disgust for the basket.

"You don't want to play, Monsieur Julius?" said Jabouille.

"No thanks."

"Would you like me to tell you a story?"

"If you want."

"I haven't yet told you mine."

It seemed that sleep was creeping up on Yvon Kerdrel, slumped in his chair.

"Here it is," said the storyteller. For a start, Jabouille isn't my name. I don't know whether I have a name, nor what age I was when I remember being unhappy—so unhappy that I still remember it today; doubtless I hadn't suffered until then."

"Probably not," said Julius.

"I remember suddenly realizing that I no longer had a father or mother. Doubtless they were dead, or had abandoned me."

A gust of voices reached the cell; Jabouille rattled the dominoes furiously. The impassive Breton seemed to be listening vaguely, half-asleep.

Jabouille continued.[9]

"I haven't told you where that was; I don't know exactly; for sure, it was in a hot country, like Senegal or Algeria; there were palm trees laden with dates and coconuts, which they monkeys plucked and threw to the ground.

"I have to go back a bit, because I need to tell you that I ran away from the house where I was beaten. It was because of the blows that I remember having taken shelter; and, small, as I was, I went into the woods. I preferred being with the animals to being beaten, and I'd always been the plaything of two or three children to whom I'd been given, and who locked me away at night with puppets and dolls in the place where they put their toys.

"Well, one morning they didn't find me; I'd left for the woods, where I went into the densest thickets. I don't know how long I was there, eating the fruit that the monkeys threw down from the trees; I don't know why

---

[9] Jabouille's story is one of two episodes that might well have been written before the novel was commenced and taken aboard as it progressed. If so, the results of this absorption helped to complicate the subsequent development of the plot in a seemingly-extraneous manner, introducing an element of scientific romance that was never to be fully developed in what is, essentially, a Suesque melodrama.

the wild beasts didn't eat me—perhaps because they took pity on me, or had better things to do.

"One day I was caught by a man accompanied by five or six blacks while I was asleep in the grass; he took me with them; I screamed in vain, they were too strong. They took me to a big hut surrounded by a garden enclosed by walls that were enormously high—or so they seemed to me.

"I was in the house of a doctor who had a lot of blacks. I thought he was very rich.

"I didn't understand why he locked me up like that, nor did I understand why he gave me a lot of drugs; I thought it was for my own good, and I obeyed, glad not to be beaten any more.

"There were rooms there full of animals there that I would have liked to see—dogs, monkeys cats, birds— but I was never allowed in. They kept arriving without the rooms ever being overfull, which was a subject of endless reflections for me; I found out why latter.

"I had a sort of band round my head; it annoyed me, but I thought it was necessary.

"One day, when I didn't see anyone any longer except the doctor, I called him my father. He began to teach me all sorts of things, and as I learned them, he took notes. I was locked in a room on my own, I don't know why. I was scared, for he was taking unimaginably good care of me, although I was almost always ill.

"I was beginning to grow up, and getting curious.

"One day, with a tool that had dropped out of my master's pocket, I pierced the wall on the side where I could hear the animals moving and crying out. In the colonies, where it's very hot, the houses are made of wood.

"Through the hole I'd made, I saw six monkeys with headbands like mine, and each band was numbered. That's strange, isn't it?"

"No," said Julius, "not very; your doctor was carrying out studies of the brain, that's all."

"Yes, but you'll see how his experiments ended."

"With the death of the patient?" Julius said.

"Listen. All the time he wasn't with me, I looked through the hole, with the result that I saw him giving lessons to the monkeys. He was trying to make them talk. He made signs to them that they made them to him. But one would have thought that the poor beasts were afraid of him, and I wasn't very reassured either.

"One day, he picked up number one to take it away. The monkey was trembling all over; its teeth were chattering.

"Two or three days later, it was number two's turn, and so on.

"The more he took away, the more the animals trembled when they saw him.

"When there were only two left, I got frightened—so frightened that I decided to run away. I was number 16, you see, and the two monkeys 15 and 17.

"I was small and the widow was high up, but I was too scared to stay. While I was looking at the window, those devilish monkeys, who weren't asleep either, spotted the hole and began to work at it with their teeth and fingernails to enlarge it.

"Believe me or not but, young as I was, the intelligence of those unfortunate beasts struck me. One night, we were busy, them gnawing away without making a sound—without making a sound, Monsieur, the brave animals!—and me saying to myself: *Just as long as he doesn't come!* when he came.

"In fact, I heard his footsteps in the house, where nothing else was making a noise. The hole was big—he was going to see it! I had an idea. I covered it with the little board that I put on my knees to write to his dictation while he was teaching me. It went dark in the monkeys' room; I heard a groan; he came out again; there was only one of them left, which sighed like a human.

"Then I took the board away, and the last monkey and I, both trembling, looked at one another through the hole.

"It was the monkey that had the most courage; it gnawed away again until it could get through and explore my room, seeking with its animal instinct for a way out.

"I understood that it wanted to make a hole in the outer wall, and I began to make a point of leverage with my tool. Fortunately, in those places, everything is lightly-built; there was soon a second hole, on which I worked with all my might, beside the monkey, which was gnawing away like a rat.

"Shortly after daybreak, we both got out. I've always thought that it was its own safety that the monkey had in mind in that expedition, for once outside, it gave me the slip, as a man would have done. I understood that it had not had enough to praise in its master to want another one.

"Once outside, I caught my breath, but I was far from being out of danger; there was a wall around the establishment; it was high, and the only door was locked tight.

"While I looked round, plastered against the wall— for I was far from feeling safe—a shadow passed over the wall; it was my monkey.

"Only a few minutes had gone by when a second shadow scaled the wall in the same place, propitious because of a big lock that could serve as a foothold for an agile animal. Immediately, though, the master himself, chasing the escaped victim, opened the door and ran outside.

"Through that open door I reached the forest, trembling like a hunted beast.

"This time, I was determined not to be caught again, and yet I sold myself—but that was to get out of the country.

"I thought that if I got on board a boat they wouldn't throw me into the sea, because it would be in front of too many people; the idea was to remain hidden long enough that I couldn't be taken back to shore. I'd noticed people going out in boats to sell fruit to ships at anchor. I succeeded in slipping on to one of these boats with other children; I'd succeeded in undoing the strap securing my headband. I hope that the poor monkeys were as fortunate.

"My clothes were in tatters, but so were those of the other children; the ones with whom I'd jumped into the canoe left me alone. I was dark enough, although I didn't have the features of a negro, not to excite any curiosity. There are so many little black kids of whom nobody takes any notice!

"I must have had a white father, but my mother was black for sure; I'm almost black myself.

"Once aboard the ship, I hid behind crates of biscuits, and made a hole in one of them in order to have something to eat.

"They didn't find me until the ship was a long way out at sea. 'What's this?' said a sailor, pulling me out of a crate in which I'd gone to sleep while eating a biscuit.

"I was lucky; I'd happened on a French ship and people had always spoken French to me.

"I was able to reply, but they didn't believe me, and even today, when I tell the story, they call me a liar..."

Hearing a new gust of voices, Jabouille shuffled the dominoes.

"In the end, they had to keep me; I became a cabin-boy, a sailor, all that devil of a life; one day, though, in a cyclone, falling off a parrot-ladder, I hurt my back, and then, another catastrophe, I was married. It was necessary to feed the kids, and a woman's work doesn't amount to much at the end of the month. I wasn't fit; one day, when the kids were moaning with hunger, the wife said to me: You have to do something, no matter what—and here I am! Isn't my story incredible?"

"No," said Julius. "Nothing seems incredible to me any more, not even being still alive tomorrow morning."

"I know a story more incredible than Jabouille's," said the Breton, who had not yet spoken. "It's a story of escape in Russia. Those Russian devils, you know, even send accomplices to the executioner."

Once again, Julius thought about Olaff.

"Let's hear about these Russians," he said.

"Well, it's about a man who was commonly known as Grizzly, like an old bear, and sometimes Medvenik, like a bear-cub; all languages are used there, there wasn't a name for a bear that he wasn't given. Now, Grizzly had a friend who was in prison..."

The rumor in the square grew louder; suddenly the voices fell silent; they were beginning to nail the scaffold together.

Yvon continued: "This resembles my comrade's adventure somewhat, in that there's also a question of scientific experiments, but it's not the same. Pierre, the prisoner, had carried out hundreds of them on Grizzly: they were concerned with electricity, magnetism—in sum, all the sciences whose sanctuaries people are trying to penetrate.

"Nihilist youth is knowledgeable; a day will come when it will demolish cannon with electricity, among other things.

"Pierre had discovered that the man guarding him was a cataleptic; the idea came to him of playing double or quits with his life. The night before the execution, he took care to appear sufficiently exhausted that he wasn't put in shackles, but not so much that the ceremony would be postponed; in sum, he showed that he was fit enough to be hanged.

There was only one thing that Pierre was afraid of, with respect to his plan, and that was being left alone that night, which would thwart his intentions, Chance favored him. He expected to be hanged every day. What if it were this time? Well, one mustn't complain. But to attempt escape pleased him, especially by that means.

"Pierre was a highly-prized individual; fortunately for him; he was closely watched. While chatting about one thing and another—as we're doing—the conversation turned to science.

"'You're an intelligent man,' he said to his guard. "I'd be happy to show you a curious experiment, but it has to be now, for I can scarcely count on tomorrow.'

The guard straightened up, swollen with pride.

"'You know that people are very interested in alternations of personality?'

"The muzjik opened his eyes wide, having no understanding at all of what alterations of personality were.

"'This is what it is: you're you and I'm me; well, I can make you feel, simultaneously, what we're both experiencing—you, who are guarding me, and me, who wants to get away.'

"'That would, indeed, be curious, but it's impossible.'

"'On the contrary; it's very easy; a Frenchman, Dr. Camuset,[10] observed it some years ago; serious experiments have been carried out, in England especially, and they've been done in France on natures exactly like yours.'"

Julius and Jabouille, captivated for different reasons, were staring at Yvon. In the street, they were still hammering nails in.

The tall blond resumed: "The muzjik listened will all ears, gazed with all eyes—and gazed so intently that he was hypnotized, as they say, and, under Pierre's influence, thinking that he was Pierre himself, lay down placidly in the prisoner's bed and let the latter leave, no less placidly, in his guard's uniform and with his keys.

"When morning came, the muzjik was still asleep; his awakening wasn't exactly pleasant, but he got away with a few cudgel-blows and the loss of his job, the doctors having suggested that he had been put to sleep by means of a poison.

"That's short—I'm not a storyteller."

"It's even more incredible than my story," said Jabouille.

"You think so?"

---

[10] A Dr. Camuset, who might or might not have been the ophthalmologist George Camuset (1840-1885), was one of several physicians to examine Louis Vivet, a patient at Bonneval who was put forward as one of the first examples of what would now be called multiple personality syndrome, and published a paper on the case in 1882.

"Is it possible for us to believe one another?"

"That can be seen every day, at the Salpétrière, Saint-Anne and Bicêtre; the doctors can do it whenever they wish."

"But the muzjik wouldn't have let it happen."

"But the muzjik had an extremely nervous and impressionable nature."

Yvon was holding Jabouille under the electricity of his gaze; to Julius' great surprise, Jabouille ended up going peacefully to sleep, so perfectly hypnotized that, like the muzjik, he obeyed in an automatic fashion, undressed himself, lay down in the prisoner's bed and meekly turned his face to the wall. Hastily, Julius put on Jabouille's clothes, leaving his own next to the bed, as was his custom.

At three o'clock in the morning two new agents came to relieve Jabouille and Yvon; they were to accompany the patient.

The exchange was made with few words.

Julius stepped over the threshold of the cell rapidly. One of the newcomers said to Yvon: "Your pal's in a hurry!"

"Yes, his kid's ill," Yvon said, leaving at a calm and even pace.

Yvon and Julius followed the sinister corridors, and emerged into the street, when Julius was able to see the scaffold, whose mechanism was being tested by the assistants. The blade glistered in the mist between the red arms.

The sound of the beehive emerged from the crowd waiting for the condemned man.

Without saying a word to him, Yvon took his companion to the Gare de Lyon, where he bought two tickets, and they were a long way from La Roquette when the governor, accompanied by this usual entourage, went into the condemned cell.

"He's not awake yet," said the agents, who had refrained from disturbing the sleep of the man they believed to be Julius.

Jabouille was unable to emerge from his magnetic sleep for several hours.

That was that for the lovers of executions. A good deal of trouble was taken to cover up the affair—as if it were a crime to let a man escape! The rumor was spread around that Julius' punishment had been commuted to forced labor for life at the last moment, but the story got around in spite of everything; it was told and retold by Jabouille, with exaggerations, with the result that the poor devil was committed to Charenton, where such strange things were successfully tried on him that a doctor succeeded in keeping him at the disposal of the Faculty. The form given to his brain by the headband worn in his infancy offered a further attraction to the investigations of science. No one had seen a similar head; he was pampered, his skull sold in advance.

Jabouille had less to mourn in his new situation less because his wife and children were not suffering. An unknown hand had come to their aid—another of those Russian devils!

No more was seen of Yvon than of Julius, for hidden under the name of Yvon, the Breton agent, was Mikhail Roskoff, Olaff's friend.

VI. Saint-Lazare

Saint-Lazare has been described many times. Eugène Sue and many others have depicted the long corridors of the old cloister, the courtyards with fountains and meager trees, whose trunks are covered with leprous moss, in the shade of high walls: trees that spring charges, even so, with foliage and birds' nests.

We shall not talk about the buildings, but the inhabitants of that warehouse of misery, where the sidewalk and the prison continually vomit over one another.

Whoever has entered it will come back! Do you think that respectable folk will give work to women who emerge from Saint-Lazare? There are, it's said, charities to aid these unfortunates; that's a drop of water in the sea. They go in and come out in human tides; one is obliged to work for two or three per thousand—which doesn't prevent people from saying: 'They're idlers! Let them work!' Where, though?

After Julius's judgment, Diana Borelli and the Irishwoman found themselves in Saint-Lazare, among those who were to be redistributed to the Centrales.[11] Separated during the entire investigation, they were brought together to hear sentence passed. They waited,

---

[11] The term Centrale is nowadays most commonly used with reference to power stations, but in 1886 it was the name given to a number of prisons to which inmates of Saint-Lazare— primarily used as a holding facility—were transferred. Louise Michel was transferred to the Centrale de Clermont from Saint-Lazare in the course of the sentence during which this novel was written.

gathered with others, for their turn to come to be transferred.

Sometimes, one goes to the Centrale immediately after sentencing; on other occasions, the departure is delayed, either because a prisoner is ill, because her family finds a way of delaying the departure, or in case of appeal.

Diana and the Irishwoman were in good health; neither had entered an appeal; they had no protection, no family capable of deferring their departure; on the other hand, they had a protection in the continual preoccupation of the man with the round eyes.

The effect of that was the same. For a long time he invented a thousand intrigues to keep them within arm's reach. Several times, cakes arrived for them, no one knew from where. For that reason, they refused them. De Gore soon ceased his attempts, fearing that he might endanger himself.

Georges told her companion how, raised in male clothing by a professor at the University of Oxford, she had believed him to be her brother until the day of her marriage; how he had left without giving her any more explanation that the Irish nationality of her mother She had heard no further mention of her adoptive father. Why? She had no idea, but if he was in hiding, it was because it was dangerous for him to do otherwise. She had not revealed his name at the trial, and took that of Cardenio, who had generously given her papers to save her life and that of her child. With regard to the name of Georges, by which the Irishman had called her, her sad features had left no doubt.

She had tried to explain her past, but she was in agreement with Odream only with respect to the name. Those explanations found the judges all the more incredulous because the Irishman had talked about a daughter of ten or eleven, and the brasserie waitress had a much younger son. It was obviously not worth the trouble of wasting time on her crazy story.

The name, however, had encountered someone it interested: Doctor Gaël, a white-haired physician with eyes full of light, whose age might have been between forty and forty-five—it was impossible to tell, because he sometimes seemed young and sometimes old, as if miraculously.

Where had he got that name, which sounded like a pseudonym? If he had been a vagabond he would have been sent, by virtue of that fact, to find a new pseudonym in a prison number—but he was a scientist, and scientists have many privileges, even that of being often mistaken, like all infallible people.

Diana could not count anyone in the world who might be interested in her; death had separated her from her mother, and she dreaded hearing at any moment of the execution of her brother. The darker the prison was, the more she hid herself there, like a wounded animal in its lair. No one was waiting for her; it did not matter whether she was put in one prison or another, whether she was condemned to twenty years or one, or for life; there was no one to be saddened by her absence.

The Irishwoman, imagining her child lost in the world, as gentle and timid as a bird, thought that she alone could find him; it was therefore necessary for her to get out.

There had been a search, she was told, but a search like those carried out for the children of unfortunates. Are there not always enough of them, if not for their mothers? Who, if not her, would go about it with passion, and pick up the trail from the slightest trace, like a bloodhound?

As for her husband, rediscovered so strangely, she did not doubt that she could save him—but the child first, the lost child all alone in the world.

Her daughter was dead—at least, she believed so—and her son, born scarcely four months after her husband's execution, so puny that he did not seem to be seven years old, had only lived thanks to her cares.

At Saint-Lazare that night, all the cells were full; there had been a police sweep, and the station had been relieved by the warehouse: sweepings of girls from the sidewalks and vagabonds from underneath the bridges, and sweepings from the drinking-dens and dives. So there were distinct types of various sorts there, ranging from the poor working-girl thrown on to the streets by her employers with a twelve- or thirteen-year-old daughter, who had made a tent with her ragged shawl between two heaps of wood on a construction site, to the brazen hussy who robbed imbeciles and emptied the pockets of swells.

Night-lights set veiled dots of light here and there, and in the calm dormitory whispered conversations are struck up everywhere; everyone has found her group; attractions exist there as elsewhere.

The fat black girl who rolled back and forth in the Brasserie du Bel Escholier is at the back of the room; the two Alsatian women occupy the beds next to hers.

"Don't go selling me out," says the black girl, "patriots that you are. Mustn't slander people—especially those who have the means to cut your throat."

This appreciation had a considerable effect on Frauchen and Rosen; they trembled, without daring to look at one another, not knowing whether the other might want to spill the beans."

"I'm sure you've already done it! Let's see, Rosen, what did the examining magistrate ask you just now?"

"Wheter the liddle girl came alone."

"What did you say?"

"Dat she came alone."

"Imbecile! And you, Frauchen?"

"Dat she came wit a lady."

(Rosen had not wanted to make the same mistake as Frauchen; they were both afraid of the black girl.)

The reply was the same: "Imbecile! You should always say that you don't know. What can you do with simpletons like you. You're trembling as if you were about to be murdered."

There was good reason, in fact, for the accusation hanging over them was terrible; the fat woman had delivered a little girl about ten years old to the "House of the Veiled Woman." (It goes without saying that the veils in that establishment were made of tulle and that its name had a double meaning.) She had enticed the child to the brasserie under a pretext and had told her to go with the old lady who was to take her. The affair had come to light because the little girl had escaped on the way and couldn't be found; the child had no one to reclaim her, though. She had been seen at the railway station; that had made a noise, and that had come back to the damned brasserie. The fat woman and the others had been arrested, but the old lady seen with the child had not been found.

Rosen and Frauchen were sad and nostalgic; they wanted to smell the new-mown hay and the bitter odor of hemp, and see the wheat undulating in the wind—but it was over, they wouldn't see any of it again, because the business was serious and the fat black girl was thinking of turning them in, giving herself the excuse that they could stand the charge better than she could.

The unfortunate waitresses were afraid, listening to her; they suspected that she had already made presumed revelations to drop them in it, but were obedient even so.

"Hey, Gribouille, how did you get nabbed," said one vagabond to another.

"I was sleeping on the ground with my kid in my arms, curled up like a cat under a tree in the boulevard. Someone grabbed me by the leg; I struggled but there were too many; they grabbed me, I defended myself and here I am."

"What have you done with the kid?"

"He's nearly three; they took him away; he's at the foundling home with a little collar round his neck to identify him, like a dog. Poor dog, eh? What did you do?"

"There was no bread in the house; the old man didn't dare say that he was hungry, which was breaking my heart—and no work, nothing. I went out, went into the baker's, picked up a nice soft loaf; he didn't want it, poor fellow, and while I was begging him to take it, a whole gang turned up to arrest me. I've been in prison for a fortnight."

"And the old man—what's become of him?"

"He's dead. He had a fit when I told him I'd taken it, and the squad that turned up afterwards finished him off. It was the baker who's told them where we live, spouting like a whale. I don't know where in pauper's field they've buried the poor fellow—I was at the station. I'm waiting to be sentenced now."

Others:

"Damn it, do I have to wait here? I've got a living to earn. What was I supposed to do when an old pig of a man invited me into his carriage, one day when I was carrying a load of washing bigger than me? I didn't come out of the damned rattletrap as I went in, that's for sure. He must make a habit of it, because that damnable doll of a coachman went along as softly-softly as if he'd been carrying God himself. The only thing missing was the bell to tell the passers-by to kneel down. In the meantime, he was busy martyrizing me, with the blinds lowered. 'If anyone hears you scream,' he said to me, 'I'll kill you; if you say nothing, I'll give money to your parents and protect them.'

"'What did he give them?'

"Four loaves of bread that he told me to give them, while throwing down a coin for me on a dark street corner, and then, 'Use your whip, coachman!' I never saw him again. Since that time I haven't had a taste for anything; I've done nothing but hang about under streetlights and beat the quarter to find a mark who'll give me what I need so that my pimp doesn't give me a beating—for I had to find a pimp right away."

"How long ago was that?"

"Four years."

"You're only sixteen, with the face you've got, the red nose and two teeth missing and the voice of a frog?"

"That's what I said—and two kids into the bargain."

"What have you done with the kids?"

"Is it the same at the foundling home as for dogs?"

"Why were you picked up?"

"Some blokes called me for a session, which they said was velvet but turned out to be a con; it was a matter of press-ganging some mug. It seemed as if the thing was going smoothly; I ran off; they shouted after me, seeing that I was getting away from the fellow who'd got me into it, and pulled out to sea. The mug was still on the water's edge. It's me that'll be put to the question, and I'll spill what I know."

"I did well," said a thin woman with dark circles round her eyes, responding to the thought that was torturing her. "I'd rather be underground than under the street-lights."

The woman turned her face to the wall, realizing that she had spoken aloud, and in the shadows, torrents of tears, as hot as a rainstorm, moistened the bedclothes that she put over her face.

"Well, what's up with her?"

"What did you do well, old woman?"

"You can see that she's a lady; Madame's not going to answer."

"Perhaps she's Charlotte's pimp's girl-friend."

Suddenly comprehending, she turned round; her face, covered in tears, glistened in the wan light of the night-lights, as if it had just emerged from underwater.

"What I did was to strangle my daughter, in the middle of the street, in broad daylight; she wasn't sixteen. I killed her because young louts had debauched her and she wanted to lead the life that you do. Yes, I did well; she's finished with the shame of it!"

The old woman's voice sounded the tocsin in the darkness and the silence; they heard it rolling through the corridors, punctuated by lugubrious intervals, falling to a curt plaint.

There was a long silence.

"Ah, if the judges only knew!" said a vagabond.

A burst of laughter responded—terrible laughter mingled with sobs.

"What have they ever known, the judges? What do we matter?"

"Is someone ill?" asked a nun, through the peep-hole.

"No, no one!"

She tapped the door with her key to call for silence, and the sound of her slippers faded away in the long corridor. On hearing the sister's voice, an old woman with a face as hollow as a crescent moon had taken out an enormous rosary and was telling the beads while moving her thin lips. When the nun had gone she continued muttering, while following the train of her thoughts—through her life, since the distant epoch when, enveloped by effluvia that were mysterious and proud at the same time, she had dreamed of Madame de Chantal[12] and founded in her imagination the Order of Divine Consolations, for which she had issued furious propaganda until the moment when, encountering a rich heiress similarly gripped by mystic love, the young woman had associated herself with her projects.

They had not remained long in invisible consolations; there were too many visible ones around them. The young woman was an orphan; she reached her majority; she could dispose of her wealth. At the sight of the large properties, the banknotes swelling the Russian leather wallet, the diamonds in the old jewel-boxes handed down by ancestors, a rapid transformation had taken place in Madame Thérèse; she had evolved into a shady businesswoman whose mysterious effluvia were no longer anything but a transparent cover for deception. The results of quests made among right-thinking people

---

[12] Jeanne de Chantal, the founder of an order of nuns in the 17th century; she was subsequently canonized.

and the orphan's fortune were swallowed up in the same abyss. The operations soon became so fraudulent that Madame Thérèse and Mademoiselle Kergaël were now lying in one of the dormitories of Saint-Lazare, one dominated by the baneful influence of the other, both having descended from the heights of dream into the sewer of swindling.

Sleep came.

Confidences were exchanged in lower voices, and silence finally fell. A wind of fear had passed over their heads with the old woman's story. Who could say that she had done wrong? Yes, better to strangle one's child in broad daylight than let her drag herself endlessly through the sewers of the prison, from sidewalk to furnished hotel, from sweep to sweep, from net to net.

Only two prisoners were not asleep.

"Diana," said the Irishwoman, "you're not thinking of leaving?"

"No, I know now that my brother's sentence has been commuted to forced labor. I'll get out before him—but I confess that I'm waiting impatiently for a letter from him."

The following morning was a day of joy at Saint-Lazare (for those to whom joy comes easy).

An old spinster, who had come modestly every day to bring what garments she could, and sometimes jobs (though that was rare), had brought two of her friends with her, with a few clothes for the women getting out, and those unfortunates obtained hope for the morrow; properly dressed, perhaps they would not be thrown out of the workshops where they went to ask for employment. They forgot the main thing. "What about the certificates, then? Don't you think we know where's you've come from" Farewell work, then! There are many charities that occupy themselves with female prisoners, but as we've said, there's only work for a tiny fraction—the drop of water in the ocean.

Statistics establish that there are in France nearly forty thousand known blind people, perhaps as many or more unknown—and the establishments that aid them have eight hundred places available. If it were only thus for female prisoners! But there's no comparison.

While the old woman was passing through the workshops with her two companions, an armored carriage pulled up in the courtyard. Ordinarily, convoys of prisoners left early in the morning. This time, dispatches had been exchanged with various administrative offices; in order to make room for further sweepings that were about to be delivered to Saint-Lazare, they could only be given the places left empty by those leaving, and there are times in the tide of misery when everything overflows: vagabonds chased from the shelters for which they can't pay; the unemployed living from day to day until they strike a vein of employment; the unfortunate who steal in order not to die of starvation.

Within these miseries, epidemics of crime are propagated; there are seasons when the sap rises in all the appetites sharpened by eternal hunger; then, so much the worse for the street-walkers; by virtue of their estate, they will be mixed up in that flourishing of crime, which extend like ripe wheat-fields before the scythes of the law.

One could say that each crime sprouts in clusters, so much are they the product of circumstances, epochs and environments. Poverty chases human flocks toward death or prison. It lays siege to towns in which bread and work are scarce; those who have children nourish them as they can; every human agglomeration becomes the raft of the *Medusa*!

One of those moments had arrived; they have scarcely ceased since. Thus, the appeal made to the Centrales to take long-term prisoners would go on for long time; they climbed into armored carriages that headed for those prisons.

The last two to be called were Diana Borelli and the Irishwoman, who had allowed herself to be recorded under the name of Luiza Cardenio, which they stubbornly insisted on attributing to her. Her papers bore that name; she allowed herself to be accused of lying, fearing to comprise her husband; she imagined, the poor woman, that he would get out of a madhouse more easily than a prison.

Diana, who had already climbed into the carriage, wondered why her companion had said goodbye to her. They were still calling room corridor to corridor and cell to cell: "Luiza Cardenio! Luiza Cardenio!"

Might she have got away? Diana wondered.

They called for a long time.

Slowly following the old woman and her two companions, a deaconess with blue-lensed spectacles over her lowered eyes, her face hidden beneath the enormous pleats of a headdress, forming a veil, her hand religiously pulled back into her sleeves, was marching at a steady pace, saluted by all the personnel.

Where the Devil have I seen that face before? the governor asked himself, as he watched her leave.

Once at the prison gate, the deaconess darted an anxious glance at the liberty filled with ambushes that presents itself to fugitives, suddenly drew herself up to the full height of her svelte figure and nimbly disappeared, without attracting the attention of those she was following.

Only Diana, who had seen the Irishwoman put on her black clothes with magical swiftness, could have revealed where the poor woman had gone.

On searching for the Irishwoman, the clothes that she had abandoned for the black costume were found in the little wood-hole where she had dressed. They remembered the deaconess. The search for Georges was widened; she was already long gone.

It is since that time that nuns are no longer allowed to enter Saint-Lazare without a pass; this was ten or twelve years ago.

Georges marched without stopping, taking endless side-roads; the news or her escape would spread; she had to change her clothes or she would be recaptured.

Why had she not kept her clothes on under her black robe? That was the thought that was obstinately fixed in her mind.

She had fifteen francs with which to buy a few rags, but she would have been sold out by the merchant from whom she have bought them; it was, however, necessary that she should not be recaptured. To wait an hour, or a minute, would be seal her doom; her description must already have been issued, but she wanted to search for her child, and then to liberate her husband, and would stop at nothing.

Confronting the danger, she forced herself to be calm, took off her head-dress in a dark place and put it in her pocket, into which her blue spectacles had vanished long before; her plaited hair seemed decent; one might have taken her for a housewife a few paces from her dwelling; she always gave the impression of living near-by. With her thick black hair she no longer resembled the deaconess of a short while before; her stature had changed, bent over as she was, in order to seem less tall. With a pin in each of her broad sleeves there was no longer anything remarkable about her costume. She bought a basket at a street-corner, and with the leisurely pace of a good housewife going to the market, resumed her aimless walk.

Darkness finally fell: a rainy night; that was lucky.

At the same pace, Georges continued walking through the maze of new and old streets, while the whole of Paris was being searched for a deaconess or an uncloistered nun. The idea that she might have thrown away her head-dress did not occur to anyone; it was always a person dressed in that manner who was sought. Bare-headed, with her basket on her arm, Georges passed in front of numerous agents; so far as everyone was concerned, she was a woman who lived in the vicinity of the place where she was seen.

But where could she stop? Nowhere, until she had found a suitable place.

Perhaps chance would favor her. Unfortunately, chance is capricious. Who could tell whether she might find generous hearts to help her? She wasn't counting on it, preferring to rely on her courage and luck.

Near the Rue de la Huchette Georges paused for breath. There is something of the tranquility of the tomb in that dust-filled morsel of Old Paris left in the new. The houses have the air of an old etching; one might think that one were living in the past. Centuries-old rats turn white there in peace in unknown redoubts. If there were only as many for vagabonds.

Was she eventually going to find a hotel in order to spend the night there safely? Even that was doubtful. A human being can't find a refuge as easily as a rat.

Georges didn't feel tired. It seemed to her that she was about to find her child; she continued walking at a steady pace, as if her were ahead of her.

In the darkness, vaguely interrupted at intervals by wan street-lights, she continued following streets that were now deserted. Georges had not eaten since morning; she was no longer thinking about anything but the regular stride whose movement her legs had mechanically taken on. Even the idea of seeking shelter had disappeared. She was walking in her sleep.

Suddenly, she collapsed, her body inert, her thoughts swallowed up.

She had fallen in the doorway of one of the oldest houses in the Rue de la Huchette. It was not a small bell, but a veritable church bell, whose rope was caught up by the fall of that heavy body, abandoned like a lifeless corpse.

The sound of that bell had reverberated inside. An old woman came running, and uttered a scream so piercing that a tall old man, as stiff as a poplar in December, arrived in his turn. He was calm, not even curious.

"What is it?" he said.

"Look, Monsieur! A sick woman has fallen on the doorstep just as she was ringing."

"Help me to carry her into the drawing-room."

Without waiting for his housekeeper's help, the old man picked Georges up, like a sleeping infant, from the threshold.

The house, small and similar to a ruin, had neither a concierge nor tenants. Doctor Gaël and his aged housekeeper were its only inhabitants, which looked from a distance like a mausoleum stranded among the living.

Georges was laid down on an old sofa.

"Get me some light, Madame Basis," said the doctor, examining the sick woman who had arrived so strangely.

In spite of his self-control, a shiver ran through him. *Can the summons of the will travel through prison walls?* he asked himself.

The Irishwoman came round slowly; a glance cast around told her that she was in the home of a physician. She realized that she had walked until her strength gave out. She must have been picked up. Where? She no longer knew.

"Thank you, Monsieur," she said to the doctor whom she could only made out vaguely at her bedside, so careful was he to hide his face.

"Don't talk yet," he said. "Rest."

His voice was emotional. Madame Basis no longer recognized her master's voice; she had seen him tremble for the first time, but, perceiving the sick woman's face, she fled in fear, dropping her candle.

"You're mistaken, Madame Basis," he said, in a tone more imperious than a command. "Not a word of any of this."

To whom would she have said anything? No one other than patients and scientists crossed the threshold.

The old woman, accustomed to considering her master as the Devil in person, obeyed fearfully; it was that same fear that had attached her to him for thirty years and more. It's true that Dr. Gaël was good and benevolent, whenever his interest in science did not demand that he was otherwise, but, oh my God, if it were in the interests of science to exterminate the entire world, he would have tried without the slightest remorse.

That fanatical scientist, however, had a tender heart in the depths of the granite breast where he stifled that terrible passion for knowledge. How many things he had done in order to know! In his long life there had been sublime deeds, and many crimes, with that sole aim. He was not proud of the former and never repented of the latter.

"Drink this, my child," he said to Georges, giving her a sedative that ought to plunge her back into sleep, but a reparative sleep this time. He picked up the candle himself and lit it again before the old woman calmed down.

"Now, Basis, you can go to sleep; I'll stay up with the patient."

Madame Basis was asking herself: "Is that what he calls the dead now? Isn't he going to throw her into his alembics, the old sorcerer? Or will she carry him away to her tomb?" She was also wondering whether the poor man might not get cold, the night was so glacial; she threw some coal on to the fire, put a cup of black coffee on the night-stand to warm him up a little and tiptoed away, as stiffly as if she were made of wood.

She got into bed, where, as usual, she pulled the bedclothes over her head, thinking that her master was the Devil himself—which didn't prevent her from harboring a thousand anxieties on his behalf. Old as she was, she had some way to go to reach the doctor's age.

As soon as he was alone with the sick woman, Dr. Gaël picked up the candle and studied her attentively. *This is the second time I've saved her!* he thought. *The impossible happens—it's the only thing that does.*

His mother had been almost that age, and resembled her closely enough to be mistaken for her, when she died. A memory was tearing the old man's heart beneath the impassive envelope in which he was wrapped; he looked at the sleeper for a long time.

What am I going to do now that hazard or will-power has brought her back to me? Isn't all affection a shackle? Unless Georges can help me in my research; she was a scientist once. Why did that accursed Irishman take her away from me?

He counted the minutes on the old clock with the sonorous chime, which slowly sounded the hours.

Suddenly, there was a loud noise in the street. It was a girl who, having had the bizarre idea of putting on a white head-dress, was being pursued and arrested as being the Irishwoman.

"It's her! It's her!" cried voices breathless with fatigue and raucous with emotion as they surrounded her, excited by the hunt for the human beast.

A sly smile passed over the doctor's face. Three o'clock in the morning chimed. The Irishwoman stirred.

Doctor Gaël moved closer to the bed. "Georges, my dear," he said, softly.

She uttered a cry, looked at him in astonishment, and threw her arms around his neck, weeping.

"Father! Why have you abandoned me for such a long time? How good you are to have saved me—you'll save them too, won't you?"

"It wasn't me; chance anticipated my desire to save you; you came here as if called—and perhaps you were."

"I went straight ahead like a hunted beast; I fell down, exhausted, and I don't know how you came."

"It was you, poor child, who stopped at my door. We won't part again, now. Science will reclaim you."

"Kind Father! There are beings dearer to me than science."

"That's the problem," said Gaël, gravely.

She told him about her escape, and then repeated, confidently: "We'll save my husband! You'll help me to find my poor child, won't you?"

"Your daughter? I forgot about her."

"My daughter's dead; it's a matter of a poor child born four or five months after the Irish insurrection, in which I thought my husband had perished.

"My daughter had been demanded by the O'Patrick family, but I was afraid; I refused; perhaps they were thinking about the diamonds; my daughter had lost them. I fled, madly, with my children; the more they sought Ellen, the more frightened I was; perhaps they would have killed me. I took her away, but she died all the same. I took refuge with them on the far side of the Pyrenees; we were ill, and were put into a kind of isolation hospital for foreigners in Barcelona.

"Our clothes were in tatters; we were stricken with typhus, scurvy and all the maladies of poverty. I didn't even see her buried. When we arrived they'd placed the children in the Niño Jésu dormitory and me in the Santa-Fernanda ward. They didn't return her to me when I left. My daughter is dead, and now, how am I going to get the other back? Almost crippled by rickets, unrecognizable to anyone but me, my poor little James, as frail as a bird, without care or nourishment."

(She had no doubt that she would find him.)

The doctor was no longer listening; his thoughts were going back to past times—as far as one of his last scientific crimes, for which his remorse was non-existent except in cases of failure; in the opposite event, it seemed to him that the sacrificed individual was the seed of an immense, infinitely-multiplied sheaf.

Having let Georges talk for a little while without interrupting her, the old man said to her: "Can you tell me exactly when you were in the isolation hospital?"

"Two years ago."

"Was your daughter blonde or brunette?"

"She had black hair."

"And the little boy?"

"He's red-haired—a yellowish red with glints of old gold. Bushy hair."

"That's good—you rest, and let me think." He addressed her as *tu*, as before.

Georges looked at the doctor in astonishment. That astonishment would have changed into fear if she had known that, at the time when Ellen was in the Niño Jésu ward of the children's hospital, it was him, Gaël, who had been in charge of the care given to those unfortunates; he had done it with the double objective of discovering the missing link between humans and apes, and developing in advance a higher race, by inhibiting the definitive sutures of the skull and acting on its development in the direction of a vast intellectual development, by means of trials with the headbands that Jabouille had mentioned.

He had tried many other things since that time, always telling himself: *It's necessary that the sown seed rots in the furrow to bring forth the sheaf, and that sheaves without number would ripen in the summer sun; it's necessary that the grape is thrown into the press, in which the wine mingles grapes without number. Thus the human seeds fall into the furrow; thus the human grapes are thrown into the press. The future will see the harvest.*

And the doctor multiplied his trials, telling himself that each sacrificed being provided a further clue. To stifle his heart required a heroism, for he would have been as well-equilibrated in terms of sentiment as in terms of intellect if he had not applied himself to stifling that half of himself. Who knows how far he would have gone? A worker only becomes more skillful by virtue of mutilating a limb.

Doctor Gaël was always accompanied in his peregrinations by the old housekeeper Basis, whom he had taken on in Senegal and who had never left him thereafter. Those two individuals had become necessary to one another, the doctor by virtue of habit and Madame Basis by virtue of fascination.

In her simple ignorance the poor woman was unable to penetrate the doctor's thoughts or objective, and did not even know why she followed him, as anxiously as a dog.

While Gaël had been carrying out his experiments in molding the skulls of monkeys and children in Barcelona, Madame de Los Amos, a woman of a certain age, had introduced herself under veritable pretexts into the Niño Jésu ward more often than anywhere else. Those pretexts opened doors in Spain—caring for the sick and the burial of little angels (as she put it) who died in the hospital occupied Madame de Los Amos incessantly. She had the bodies of certain beautiful little girls reserved for appropriate burial instead of delivery to the scalpel. Ellen was one of them.

Madame de Los Amos had loved those little girls so much that she was admired for it. But once the little coffins were placed in the crypt of her ancestors—a vast and profound cellar—the great lady went furtively by night to recover the poor girls, to whom she had given narcotics, and sold them without compromising herself (since they had been declared dead) to highly placed ogres with a taste for fresh flesh. Some woke up, others passed from sleep to death.

The doctor had discovered the horrible woman's secret, unfortunately too late for Ellen, and had threatened her with the law; but she, who had discovered the secret of the headbands in her turn, denounced the doctor's methods, and he was obliged to leave Barcelona.

Perhaps, therefore, Ellen was no more dead than James; she was, like him, in the world. Her fatal beauty would have persuaded the old woman to wake her up, and the child must have been sold many times already. Gaël remembered that little "corpse" with the long black hair perfectly, whom Madame de Los Amos had just taken when he discovered the secret of the lethargies.

Sometimes, he wondered whether he was not a being as horrible as the Spanish *grand dame*, but he always replied that he was ending a few lives for discoveries that would preserve millions of others, or clarifying some obscure point of science. With his headbands he was sometimes trying to alleviate the animality of the great apes, sometimes opening a route to an enormous development of faculties. Then again, he had often carried out his experiments on subjects of vague and troubled existence, in order to spare others; he had even descended as far as plants—is sap not blood? In Senegal, he had vaccinated papayas against jaundice with the sap of other papayas; only his trees had survived the vegetable epidemic. He had electrified bananas, those strange vegetables whose clusters emerge from a bloody rent in the tree like bunches of eggs. He had electrified others— moulis—which had become phosphorescent.

His trial had succeeded. Even experiments of humans did not weigh on him anymore. As one sows seeds in various terrains, he had contrived strange crosses between animals species by artificial means—and if he had not yet done that with humans, it was not his fault; he had not despaired of doing so; only the opportunity had been lacking.

Once, in Oxford, on a winter's night, he had coldly removed a young woman from the strangers' hospital (whom he had put to sleep himself), as a beast carries off its prey, and taken her home to serve in his horrible experiments. Intoxicated by laboratory emanations, the cruelty of his experiments and a passion for science, he had attached her to the dissection-table; then, his hackles rising in horror, recognizing his crime, anticipating her awakening, he put her to sleep again in order to keep her in his power, and had interrogated her while thoroughly hypnotized during the vivisection.

Frissons ran through his flesh; fear passed through him, but he continued, without his hand trembling, to rummage in that human breast. The unfortunate woman replied to her torturer, describing her suffering. Suddenly, she uttered a howl; shivers passed through her; she expired, giving birth to a girl.

Doctor Gaël sometimes heard that scream again during the night. Although he had no remorse and believed profoundly that there was no crime in matters of science—that one had not taught him anything, which aided the remorse—he had the child brought up, and when she was returned to him at the age of six or thereabouts, fearing all dangers for her, he put her in boys' clothes. She retained them until she was seventeen. He had wanted to preserve her from any weakness of education, but above all to discover whether there was equality, inferiority or superiority of intelligence and learning between that feminine subject and the male students of the University. He only had one subject, obtained at hazard, but there was a chance, and then he would carry out other trials—he expected to have a thousand years ahead of him.

In the black races, where exercise is much the same between the two sexes, the female skeleton closely resembles that of the male. Why should it not be the same for intellectual faculties?

Georges was his adopted child and, above all, his experimental subject. She developed marvelously, becoming one of the best students in the faculty at Edinburgh. He loved her passionately—it was science that he loved in her—but events disposed of Georges' destiny in a manner very different from Doctor Gaël. A student, the Irishman O'Patrick, a dreamer, discovered that the handsome student was a woman and fell in love with her. It was noticed.

There was great emotion in the University—a veritable scandal. The affair was depicted in lurid colors, and if the two young people had not got married, the story would have spread far and wide, to the detriment of science. That, as much as the obstinacy of the young man, had prompted Dr. Gaël's decision.

The marriage was made in spite of the O'Patrick family, who wanted a dowry. The young couple took refuge on a farm in Ireland, where the former student took part in one of the frequent revolts of the starving.

As for the doctor, after the departure of his adopted daughter, he left Oxford, traveled all over Europe and settled in Barcelona, where we encountered him in the Niño Jésu, and from there, after numerous vicissitudes, came to Paris.

VII. The Red-Haired Child

In the sad solitudes of Sologne, under the black firs, in the desolate forests, there are strange pools as smooth as mirrors, scarcely troubled from time to time by a bubble of air like those that fish make as they come to the surface to breathe.

The water is dark, like the glaucous green of the Seine on the evening when it attracts. These minuscule lakes are leech-ponds.[13] Certain capitalists make millions feeding the beasts.

It's so simple to fatten leeches on living prey! Are there not toothless dogs that can do no more? Are there not old horses, exhausted servants whose bones are piercing their bristling hide? If that hide is no longer saleable, the blood is still good; the beast is allowed to graze in peace, and remakes a few liters. Then it is forced to go into the pool; and the leeches have a feast, attaching themselves to its legs, its flanks and its breast. There are great eddies in the livid water, which becomes red in places, as if it were flowering.

If the animal refuses to go into the pool, the whip and the stick reason with it; when it is not worth the trouble of being sucked several times, it is driven into deep water, where it is maintained, threatened by long poles. Its head, which is scarcely above water, trembles for a while; then, with a terrible whinny, it says goodbye to unkind nature and disappears.

---

[13] Medicine still being in a direly primitive phase in the late 19th century, there was a considerable demand for leeches, which had to be supplied...

At other times, the beast is still strong, and is worth fetching out, as long as it has the courage to make more blood. In Spain, it would be used in the arena; unable to be disemboweled by bulls, it is given to the leeches to suck, which grow fat and bring in a handsome profit. If one could do as much for all old servants, it would avoid many recriminations, wouldn't it? Perhaps they'd suffer less.

Sometimes, in spite of the lashes of the whip and the prodding of the poles, a horse that one wishes to use again doesn't want to climb back up the slope; it would prefer to get it over with—but it has to come out. Then, trembling on its limbs, its eyes full of terror, covered in blood, it stands on the bank, from which it is driven further on with strokes of the whip.

Sometimes, the guardians of these sinister flocks drive them before them like specters; they take them to eat a little grass under the fir-trees before bringing them back again.

In one of these desolate forests, on a cold April night, a poor little child is dragging his swollen and heavy feet. His garments hang down in a thousand tatters like the down of skylarks.

The night is clear, the stars shining through the branches—which almost reassures the child. Small as he is, he would barely be a single mouthful for a wolf—but on that beautiful night he would see the beasts coming; the road he has taken is broad and white, and the wolves would form dark shadows.

Weary, his feet bruised, dying of cold and hunger, the child keeps going; he's courageous, that boy—and then again, he's already old, nine years gone, although one wouldn't know it by the exiguity of his stature.

Finally, a place appears where he can rest; it's the edge of a black pool in the shadow of the fire-trees. Large stones are set there, as if for sitting on. From there, he can see in all directions, and besides, he thinks that others are in their beds.

People do sit there, in fact, but in order to guard the horses that are shoved into the pool and poked with long poles if they try to get out of the water before those that are not to be used again are finished, when they're allowed to slip under the water uttering the whinny of death. It's from there that the others are prodded.

The child sits down. Will he be able to get up again? He doesn't think so; perhaps it would be as well to let himself fall into the water; it would only take a moment and he'd be asleep forever. He thinks about that, poor thing; it's been such a long time since he slept in a bed that the watery bed is tempting.

But here comes an enormous shadow: the wolf, no doubt; a big wolf, as in the tales. The little creature, frozen with fear, waits without a cry being able to escape his throat, without trying to flee, because he can't.

The beast arrives beside him, enlarged by the shadows; it lowers its head toward the pool, dying of thirst, and raises it again fearfully; before its avid tongue there has been a movement in the water; the leeches have scented their prey.

It's a horse! The child say to himself, reassured. He calls to it in a soft voice; it's a companion, a friend; he'll no longer be afraid.

Hesitant at first—it isn't accustomed to softness— the horse advances toward the child, walking with difficulty. Lowering its head, it licks his face.

Who can tell what has occasioned the animal's affection? The child's heart breaks beneath that caress; he takes the head of the benevolent beast in his hands and weeps, placing his cheek against the animal's meager head.

It's one of the horses set free to make more blood and be used again.

Those two wretched individuals, the abandoned child and the beast condemned to feel itself being eaten alive, remain thus for a few moments; courage returns to them; they are no longer alone against the mute heavens and the unkind earth waiting, devoid of pity for anyone, for something heavy whose advent its senses.

The little boy has stood up; his thick red hair, more tangled than the horse's mane, and his face, covered with the dust of the road, have been washed by the poor beast's tongue; his tears have been drunk; they will not leave one another again—that's what the child is thinking, and perhaps the animal.

They sleep, the child between the horse's feet, leaning on his dolorous flanks, streaked with cuts.

What a beautiful night! It's nearly a year since the child spent one like it; he fled when his mother was arrested, hearing it said that he would be put in the foundling home; not wanting her to be locked up, he wanted, in his childish illusion, to try to get her out.

Imagining that he might succeed, he hid in order not to be mistaken for a stray dog that might be sent to the pound, and went on and on without knowing where, thinking about his mother, not doubting that he would see her again.

Once outside Paris, the poor child, sometimes begging for bread and bedding down in farm stables—as he had heard about in stories less sad than his own—had not been stopped; chance sometimes works that way;

one doesn't always pay attention to such a small creature; he passes by without being aware of the danger.

The animal and the child only woke up at dawn, both rested; the beast was feeling better; the child could stand up on his swollen feet; then, quite simply, as if he were its owner, the child called to his comrade, who followed him along the broad white road through the woods.

A heavy dew covered the plants, and they both drank. The child never wearied of embracing his friend, which passed its tongue over his face. They set off with their thirst quenched, bound for the unknown.

They had just discovered a few wild fruits, a treasure equally divided, when a gendarme appeared, blocking their route.

"Where are you going with that horse, child?"

"I don't know, Monsieur."

"Yes you know full well, you little wretch. You're stealing it! You know very well where you're taking it, you little brigand!"

"Monsieur, I beg you, let me have him! If you knew how he loves me!"

"Come on, no jokes, or I'll teach you to laugh."

"But I'm not laughing, Monsieur." And the child burst into tears.

"What's your name?"

"James, Monsieur."

"James who?"

"I don't know."

"Come on, let the animal go—it'll find its own way back to be sucked—and come with me."

Cutting a flexible rod with his saber, the gendarme stung the flank of the horse at a place where there was a raw wound, around which flies were buzzing.

In response to the pain, the beast galloped back along the road. As for the child, uttering a loud scream, he vanished into the thicket, from which it was impossible to retrieve him.

He's some lad from a nearby farm, the gendarme said to himself. *I should have thought of that sooner; it would be stupid to waste my time, when I only have to keep my eyes open until I see him again.*

VIII. The Irishman

Once plunged into the laboratory in which, as poor Gill[14] put it, human brains are ground up as if by a mill once they are identified as mad and furiously mad, Odream became calm, and in that calmness, felt the need to get out of there, not wishing to die, because that would have been unjust.

As if it were not always that which is unjust that must be.

His daughter must be dead; his wife had betrayed him—the child that she was dragging around with her was proof of that; everything was crushing him, but he did not want to finish there; all of his reason was in revolt.

In the profound void of his heart, human dignity has risen up. It no longer pleased him to submit to the insulting pity of which he had no need, and he felt that he had the courage to climb out of the gulf into which he had been plunged.

The day before, searching for his beloved wife and daughter, hope had almost awoken in him; that had now deserted him. So, he stood alone before the engulfment of his life; calm audacity took hold of him.

To get out of that deadly place, it was necessary to convince the physicians, the directors of the establishment, that they were mistaken about him, that he was

---

[14] The caricaturist André Gill (1840-1885), of whom Michel would doubtless have approved, for his relentless caricaturing of Adolphe Thiers. He was committed to Charenton as a lunatic in 1880.

full of reason and strength, and suffering horribly from being nailed into that coffin alive. If he did not succeed, he decided to employ cunning and make use of any means that presented themselves to escape.

Because of his artistic nature, the habit remained, no matter what the horror of the situation, of taking account of the external details of his surroundings. That calmed his mind, and relaxed him somewhat. He had seen the unfortunate lunatics looking at him pityingly, putting their fingers to their foreheads to signify that he was mad.

"Come and look at the madman," the imbeciles had yapped, while drooling, summoning the others to the peephole of is cell.

Sometimes, he heard those words echoing in the corridors in low voices. "He's going to come down, the madman; we'll run after him! Madman! Madman!" The drool splashing over the lips of the unfortunates drowned their voices in the sound of little waves. Every time the lunatics went into the courtyard to exercise, the scenes were renewed.

Scraps of visitors' conversations also reached him, rising up to his padded cell; outside, his friends, convinced that he was mad, were mourning him—which, before the public, attached the warning bell solidly around his neck. It was sometimes said that he seemed calmer, as he had never ceased to be. That gave him the impression that someone buried alive must have on hearing the earth beneath which he is to be laid fall upon his coffin.

It was necessary to put an end to the situation.

Odream had great difficulty obtaining a pen, with a little ink and some paper. Such things are freely given to a prisoner, but a madman—that's different! He might strangle himself with the pen, drink the ink or—what do I know?—stab himself with the inkwell; everything must he refused to him, since he might harm himself.

When the man is mad, they're right. But what about those who aren't?

Odream tried to talk to the celebrated alienist who supervised the establishment. The latter listened to him attentively.

Odream showed him the memoir he had written, in the hope that he would be able to make it known, about the tortures he had undergone—among others, the bromide, which had only numbed him, trapping him in a nightmare of which he could take account without being able to go to sleep. It would have required an enormous dose to triumph over his will, whose rebellion kept him on his feet.

What point was there in putting him to sleep? He wasn't mad and meant no harm to anyone; he had never lost his reason.

Why, since he was entirely rational, was he being subjected to the torture of that treatment? He could never even attain the artificial sleep into which they were trying to plunge him. He begged to be allowed to devote himself to his usual endeavors.

"Have you always had headaches?" the alienist asked him, pursuing his idea.

"I've never had headaches?"

"That can't be; that's the diagnosis."

The doctor passed on. Then, having had a sudden thought, he went back to the padded cell. "I'll take your manuscript."

The manuscript was a poignant study. and cut to the quick. The alienist reflected that the man might indeed be rational."

After all, he said to himself, *science is sometimes mistaken.*

He went back to Odream's cell then, wanting to convince himself that his patient had not been suddenly cured. The responsibility of his science was at stake. He chatted with him for a while, listening with profound attention.

Damn! he said to himself. *This could well be a cure. I've cared for him so well!*

Odream, for his part, could see himself already set free, when the physician said to him, in order to convince himself that no trace of madness remained: "Now, Monsieur Odream, will you tell me how you were hanged?" The alienist wanted to make sure that the idea of the execution had been erased.

"Gladly, Monsieur."

"Aha! So you still remember being hanged?"

"If you'll permit, Monsieur, I can convince you..."

The physician was already far away, murmuring: "These damnable madman! These damnable madmen! It's a good job I asked him about that—I was about to let him go."

Who would not have thought he was right? Would you not believe that someone who told you that he had been hanged was mad? He should have listened, though.

In his capacity as a physician and scientist, Doctor Gaël could present himself at the establishment of his fellow alienist whenever he wished.

They were two beings as unlike one another as any in the world; they made contact, however, on one capital point: science, which they both served fanatically, but very differently.

Dr. Eraste, the alienist, scrutinizing a very small part of it, without worrying how that part related to the whole, was a specialist. Dr. Gaël, without stopping at the details, grasped the whole. Both beings belonged, in terms of their character, to the strange times of alchemy, and by virtue of their discoveries, to our epoch. Science was everything for them; they would have sacrificed their own lives to discovery, and would have offered anyone else's existence if necessary.

Dr. Gaël was addressing himself to his colleague in order to save the Irishman. It was the first time in his life that he had thought about anything except scientific questions, although it is true that they were nevertheless involved.

The alienist having already had a favorable doubt, Dr. Gaël would soon have arrived at his objective, if fatality had not made Odream commit the error of mentioning his execution again.

"It's possible," said Dr, Gaël, "that the execution about which your patient speaks really did take place, but that, by virtue of circumstances..."

His colleague interrupted him; he did not want to hear mention of that item of insanity. "No," he said, "it was the man's madness." And, reflecting that insanity is contagious, he wondered: *Is he too going mad?* Looking at Dr. Gaël compassionately, he added: *Such things have been known!* And he did not want to hear any more about it.

Gaël saw that it was necessary to put it off until another occasion.

As they were parting at the main gate, a poor devil with a bewildered expression came in, in order to continue a series of interesting experiments with the alienists, one of whose subjects he was. On seeing Dr. Gaël he stopped dead momentarily, his eyes dilated by fright; then he resumed his course without saying a single word.

The poor devil in question was Jabouille. He had recognized the physician of the headbands.

"I regret," said the alienist, that the imbecile ran off like that. "I would have liked you to see one of the most curious things that are possible. One might think that his skull had been kneaded by a diabolical hand, in order to give certain cerebral lobes an abnormal development. The thing must have gone awry; there was a miscalculation, and the miserable wretch is an idiot. Someone wanted to see the advancement or retardation of the human type—I don't know which."

"Perhaps the fellow didn't have the time to finish," said Dr. Gaël, with perfect insouciance, "but he surely wanted to see the advancement and the retardation."

"What do you think of such attempts?"

"I think that no discovery has been made without throwing gold or human lives at it, but that it returns a hundredfold profit."

"I believe you're right." Not only did he believe it but he felt a certain relief in encountering a scientific authority with the same opinion, for, if he did not carry out Dr. Gaël's experiments, he carried out others, being one of those who grind up human brains now in order to preserve those of future generations.

I'll never get past the obstinacy of that accursed Eraste, the old man said to himself, who was not astonished by his encounter He had seen so many strange things in his life—and Jabouille might be useful to him in procuring Odream's liberty, which he had promised Georges.

Collectors of tulips and paintings swap specimens; why shouldn't scientists do likewise?

After returning home, Dr. Gaël wrote to the alienist:

My dear colleague,

I once studied the questions that are preoccupying you, and delved into them in such a positive fashion that my notes might elucidate certain obscure points. I didn't need to see your subject for a long time to take account of the transformations to which his brain have been subjected. The experiments were abruptly abandoned, but I can indicate the path that they followed.

I need, in exchange, your other patient Odream. I want to have him at my disposal for a few days—with a very important objective, as you shall see. Moreover, I see now that you're right in recognizing madness in his persistence in believing that he has been executed. I hope to inform you as to the man's particular case.

Your admirer and colleague

DR. GAËL

Certain people, while recognizing that they have made a mistake, also like to believe themselves infallible, although the two are scarcely consistent.

Was the alienist flattered that Dr. Gaël had come round to his opinion? He must have been, for that same evening, after receiving the missive, he put Odream into a cab, saying to him:

"My dear Monsieur, I'm taking you to a colleague who will let you talk all day long about what you say happened to you. If you're rational, you won't make any futile attempt to escape on the way; you'll await the result of his observations."

Odream promised to do so.

Indeed, said the alienist to himself, *if one could rid him of his obsession, I'd be inclined to set him free. At any rate, his case isn't very curious. I can't see why my colleague thinks it remarkable.*

Courteously, he introduced his subject to his colleague.

Odream, recognizing his wife and the Oxford scholar who had taken the place of her father, had the presence of mind to keep quiet. Georges contained herself too.

If she had only applied that strength of character to study! thought Dr. Gaël.

He gave his colleague the extremely detailed report concerning Jabouille's brain. Only he could have done that. "Fair exchange is no robbery," say misers. It's the same for all of us, passionate as we are about the unknown, and for social transformation.

To describe the admiration into which the alienist was plunged by the lucidity of the report would be impossible. He did not understand how Dr. Gaël had been able to identify so clearly the source of the cerebral alterations of a subject he had barely glimpsed.

Jabouille would have been able to tell him if, having been plunged into profound terror by the appearance of his former master, he had not been content to say: "I ran away because I was afraid."

"Afraid of what?"

"I don't know."

Irrational fear was mentioned in Gaël's report; all was well.

The alienist, returning to his colleague's house to express his high esteem for such a profound scientific observation, thought for the first time in several days about his other subject, Odream. Perhaps Dr. Gaël had cured him!

Having received the alienist's congratulations, Gaël announced that, cured or not, but on the way to recovery, Odream had run away.

All things considered, the flight of an inoffensive madman wasn't worth the trouble of quarreling with a great man. Dr. Eraste departed with an almost light heart, by virtue of having something to forgive Dr. Gaël.

He counted without so many things, the poor alienist. Rumor spread of Odream's cure, and people wanted to see him; he said that he was seriously ill, and eventually declared him to be dead. It would have been simple to admit that he had escaped, but the fear of compromising Dr. Gaël made the alienist take that course. People complained that he had not let them know about the funeral. Perhaps he could have stolen for the occasion one of the least rational of his subjects. Fortunately for him, grave political events caused Odream to be forgotten.

The unfortunate Irishman's gratitude with regard to Gaël was immense. The latter, while still quivering with the remorse that had never left him, experimented with the phenomena of suggestion at a distance that he thought he had exerted on Georges. Perhaps he was not mistaken, and no-less-extraordinary phenomena of material instinct were about to become manifest in the search for the lost child. It occurred to him momentarily—for he loved them, to the extent that he was capable of love—to tell them that Ellen too might be alive, but he wanted to see whether the instinct of the human animal, as sure as that of an animal, would divine something. Anyway, he promised to carry out his own search.

In the meantime, the man with the round eyes was also getting his bearings. With the instinct of security that drove him sniffing out those who might harm him, he was about to hurl himself, swollen with venom like the threatened viper, on the track of all those surrounding Julius, so the poor people searching for their child could not fail to encounter him.

When one has once seen a black mamba, negroes say, one finds it three times. The man with the round eyes, deadlier than the snake, was fatal, and better able to conceal himself. The opposite of Gaël, Olaff and the alienist, who would have sacrificed thousands of lives to open up new routes, he would have sacrificed the universe, apart from himself, in order to close them; while they believed they were spreading seed that might perhaps grow, he destroyed for the sake of destruction.

IX. Makaïk's Wedding

The beautiful Makaïk is marrying the handsome Yves Legonidec. All the bagpipes in Armor,[15] for six leagues around, are at the wedding-feast.

Yves and Makaïk are both twenty years old. They have loved one another for ten years, but if the baz-valan[16] had not told them that it was necessary to marry, they would have been content to dance together on holidays and think about one another, always desiring to see one another in order to exchange a few words signifying nothing at all, but which they were pleased to say to one another.

"Bonjour, Makaïk."

"Bonjour, Yves."

"Lovely weather!"

"If the wind keeps blowing there'll be bad weather this evening."

Etc., etc. And a thousand other things just as new, which their thoughts could take as reference-points.

The parents on both sides thought that the baz-valan was right.

The wedding is being held, as in the time of ancient Armorica, in a house built of wood and earth; the ancestors could have wandered in and found nothing different from two thousand years ago. In the first room, an oar (the spectral oar) was dipped in the lustral water; it's the rector who has blessed it, but it's still the druid's white

---

[15] Armor, or Armorica, was the Celtic name of Brittany.

[16] A Breton match-maker.

robe that one sees prowling under the branches he's cut by moonlight.

Legend still blows over you, Armor, with the sounds of the ocean; your sons sometimes kill us, old Brittany, but at least they think they're doing the right thing; fanatics are more upright than hirelings.

We shall have it, old Brittany! The wind of the new legend will pass over your Kernevotes[17] and your bell-ringers will make tomorrow's bard-songs resound, your blue-eyed bell-ringers with long hair tied in a ribbon.

A fire of dry branches shines in the tall fireplace; the long table is filled by guests; it is Yves Legonidec who is singing and the bell-ringers reply, but the wind is mournful, Yves' song is sad, and the bushes weep as they reply.

Yves is a visionary; he knows the legend of the tidal wave better than anyone in the world:

Biscoas den ni driménas ac ras
N'en divez avoun peglaz.[18]
(No one passes the tidal wave
Without harm or fear.)

The hero of the legend was a great-great-uncle of Yves Legonidec's great-great-grandfather, and he was given the name in obedience to the Kernevotes.

---

[17] Kernevote is a Breton term for the hawthorn; Louise Michel's poem "La Kernevote" can be read on-line. The subsequent use of the term suggests that the trees were credited with some mystic authority.

[18] I have reproduced these two lines of Breton exactly as they appear in the original. The French translation given there does not retain the rhyme, but when ballad given in full is rendered in French, it is rhymed. I have reproduced the meaning without attempting to reproduce the rhyme-scheme

Yves Legonidec, son of Jean de Guérande,
Sang as he steered straight toward the wave,
Saying: my boat is small, and the sea is great,
And the nor'wester weeps in the sky like a knell.

Yves is to marry Jennie and his heart sings
The gulf of Plogoï is yawning and roaring:
The distant wave unfurls and the wave laments
And the masses of the sea foam in the darkness.

Who cares? He cannot hear; Jennie is pink and
blonde
And the flower of the black wheat will be in her
hair.
Yves is no longer aware of the sea or the world,
They will love one another forever and grow old.

The breeze murmurs gently on the strand
The next morning, but Yves does not return.
The Ocean took him in the midst of his dream;
Without harm or fear, no one passes the tidal wave.

It was Yves himself who was singing; the bardic
song and the bagpipes were weeping when Yves had
concluded the dreamy lines of the chorus.

Bac valek a sobian harc Armor a zobras.
(My boat is small and the sea is great.)

Silence fell in the hall; a plaint was heard outside. It was the Korrigans[19] for sure; perhaps the Ankou[20] was about to pass by; everyone felt a frisson of terror. An old prophetess started to say that it would be necessary to sacrifice or save the first creature that appeared, according to whether it turned to the left or right on the threshold.

Perhaps they would have hesitated to sacrifice the first creature that appeared, for it as a child: a child with hair that as still red beneath the water that dyed it, for it was raining hard outside.

Everyone breathed more easily when the child looked unconsciously to the right, inasmuch as he could look, through the large droplets falling from his hair upon his eyes, blinded by virtue of having emerged from the darkness into the lamplight of the wedding, feeble as it was. I don't believe that they would have sacrificed him if he had looked to the left, but superstition is a powerful thing.

"I'm very cold," he said, moving toward the fire, dared with fatigue and hunger. Makaïk put him on her knee, all wet, without fear of spoiling her wedding dress.

They had saved the first creature that had come in, and the prophetess murmured: "The curse is lifted."

This time, the bagpipes sang joyfully, the bell-ringers all stood up and never had such a sonorous refrain been heard so far away.

---

[19] Dwarf-like spirits, usually imagined as malevolent, or at least mischievous.
[20] The original has "ancien Karikel," of which I can make no sense. The Ankou is the spirit of death in Breton folklore, and seems to fit the context.

Then they warmed the child in front of the fire and gave him a bowl of warm cider, while Makaïk's mother went to look for the big box of warn clothes that were now too small for the bride's younger brother, but were too large and too long for the little vagabond; he put them on all the more easily, and the way he looked in them made the assembly laugh. As he had been revived by the gentle heat of the fire and the cider, comforted by the joy that surrounded him, and especially by the good welcome, the child raised his bowl, which was not yet empty, and, remembering one of his mother's refrains, started crowing like a young cockerel:

"Erin go bragh!" It was the war-cry of green Ireland: Ireland forever!

Hands were clapped; no one knew how he came to be there.

He was so strange, with his big head, made enormous by his shock of red hair. Might he not be a child? Had he not been blown in by a gust of wind, from the heath where the Korrigans assembled in order to dance in the gorse?

That thought made Makaïk go pale.

"Where do you come from, child?" asked the prophetess.

"Far away, Madame, oh, very far away; I couldn't walk any further, and I was afraid."

"What's your village called?"

"Paris, Madame."

"Paris! Such a small child! How have you managed to come so far?"

"I don't know. I kept going forward, but I haven't come in a straight line, of course; I've been walking for a long time."

"Why didn't you stay with your parents?"

"They took Maman away, and I heard them say that they wanted to put me in the foundling home. I was scared; I ran away. I haven't seen Maman again—but I'm not a foundling, am I, since I have Maman?"

"How old are you?"

"I was about to be nine when I ran away, a long time ago. I haven't counted the months."

Nine! He didn't look any older than six, for sure. He was a dwarf.

"Have you seen the leaves return since then, or have you seen them fall?"

"Oh, that's true—I've only seen them fall." He put his head in his hands, in the reflexive gesture of a man. "It's just that it seemed like a long time."

"Who took care of you during that time?"

"No one—on the contrary, children ran after me in villages and people wanted to lock me up, because I was all alone and very small. There was only a horse that was kind to me."

"A horse? That was the Drak."[21]

"I don't know.

"It was black, wasn't it?"

"I think so."

"It was the Drak for sure. You didn't pluck a hair from its mane?"

"What for?"

"To break the spell."

"I don't know what that is."

Mingled with fear and pity, such was the arrival of the little vagabond James, wandering through the world, through the wind and the rain, and falling upon Makaïk's

---

[21] The Dragon—i.e., the Devil.

wedding. Also mingled with fear and pity was his adoption by the newly-weds.

The child did not forget his mother; every day he begged for help in finding her. They promised to do so, but with the firm intention of doing nothing—because, from the little they knew, they guessed that she had been arrested.

To be arrested, for the people of Armor and many others, is to be guilty.

The child tried to understand, but his mind refused to comprehend that his mother could have done anything wrong.

Where could she be found? Where could inquiries be made? In the prisons? They would detain him. In Paris? All alone, he knew that he would be put in the foundling home. Perhaps his mother would get out; they shouldn't have taken her; she hadn't done anything—but how would she know where he was?

Such were little James' reflections, sitting on the stones of the hearth during the long winter evenings, in the home of the young couple who had adopted him.

X. The Man With The Round Eyes

It is logical that studies proceed through successive encyclopedias.

The rage to know grips us, and at the commencement of the epoch in formation, the broadening of study can open up to avid minds the routes of tomorrow, or leave them still rooting through the monstrosities of shreds of putrefied science.

The man with the round eyes, while his entire being went back to savage ancestors, lived in the breath of our epoch. He wanted to know, as everyone wants to know, and had even had generous aspirations in his early youth, at which he laughed today, having kept to himself rather that spreading abroad the currents of intelligence and strength that were overflowing within him. Then, instead of being the center of a radiation, one is more reminiscent of a sewer in which the avidities of the mind, the strength of the will and the rapacity of the appetites accumulate.

The more broadly the being develops, the more nature completes it, the greedier it becomes; it's necessary that everything within it tries to feed it. Instead of producing it absorbs—imagination, will, flesh, brain; everything must absorbed its nourishment, at everyone else's expense.

One sees, by virtue of the laws of atavism, a wolf born among the shepherd's dogs, going back through a thousand crosses to a savaged ancestor, capriciously introduced. A white child born in a black family or a black child in a white family goes back to eras far more primitive. The man with the round eyes is no more astonishing; born in another environment, he would have been like other men of his native land; raised as he had been, he was a beast of prey with human intelligence; he took after his grandfather, in whom, in order to enrich the family, the activity of a entire race had been concentrated: a powerful vitality that was to terminate in him alone, being the last flicker of flame in an exhausted lamp.

He was to have no descendants; the past and future of his race were summarized in him; he had the covetousness, the avidity, the will of millions of generations; his intelligence, in that accursed milieu, served his appetites uniquely, and, conserving impunity, he believed that he would always have it.

An ogre, a satyr: such was the man with the round eyes at the moment when he committed the crimes of which he accused others; standing up against humanity entire, although hidden, he had only to spit out his venom.

Constrained to demand silence from Sylvain Mirbel, he had preferred to kill him—only the dead don't talk. That was the only time he had been discovered before the adventure of Julius. Tranquil on Sylvain's account, and wanting to appropriate the enormous sums imprudently displayed to him by his correspondent, he had poisoned the scarab when the opportunity presented itself, and had accused Julius; he always seized an opportunity; that was his method.

The spider, well-hidden in his web had been catching human flies in it for a long time. Although Julius' escape caused him some anxiety, no eye was fixed upon his round eyes, except for the eyes of a very simple man, a humble street-porter named Yves Kergaël, who must be a Breton.[22]

Yves Kergaël, busy almost all day long, found the time nevertheless to go to a thousand places frequented by revolutionaries. "It amuses me," he said, naively, "although I don't understand it. The theater is too expensive, and I wouldn't understand it any better."

The idea had never occurred to anyone to offer him a compliment or a reproach. The poor man was not one of those who made a noise; no one could fear that simple mind, which replied to all questions with quips.

Perhaps people might have been astonished that the quips weren't stupid, but who the devil thinks about a creature as insignificant as a street-porter, who counts for nothing?

Once, however, the man with the round eyes, turning round instinctively, felt a gaze fixed upon him.

One always feels that, the gaze.

That first time, he didn't see anyone; the second time, he perceived a creature scarcely reminiscent of a human being, walking bent over, as if his back and head formed a horizontal line, like an animal, with an enormous weight on his back, who seemed to be going on all fours.

---

[22] The surname Kergaël has already been used in the text to refer to the victim of the religious swindler in Saint-Lazare; as the reader will probably have guessed, this is a different character who has previously been glimpsed under a similar name, but I do not know whether the variation here is deliberate, or a misreading on the part of the copyist. At any rate, I shall preserve it until it is substituted in the original.

He was not the man to worry the man with the round eyes; the latter smiled at the brief anxiety that had gripped him.

The third time, when he saw the same creature behind him, it annoyed him, but it had to be coincidence.

One day, as he passed the Brasserie du Bel Escholier, which he no longer entered, out of prudence, he turned round abruptly and saw the street-porter, who was crossing the road, his back still bent like a frog, carrying his entire burden on it like a donkey. The individual calmly crossed the street.

The man with the round eyes remembered that the first time he had turned round anxiously had been in the Bois de Vincennes, and then in the Champs-Élysées, another time on, the boulevard, and this time in front of the brasserie. Decidedly, he and the person who was troubling him were traveling in the same direction. There was nothing astonishing in their paths crossing, but this was too often.

That gaze followed him, churning in his heart. Soon, it no longer left him. Then, confronted by the obsession, the madness whose advent he felt, he resolved to get rid of the street-porter. It was a long time since his last murderous venture, but he never operated in the same way twice; that would have been imprudent. Having found the means, it was his turn to look for the street-porter, but he could no longer see him anywhere.

One evening, when he was, by design, outside a popular meeting-hall, watching the swarm of black worker bees in the hive, the man with the round eyes found himself face to face with the street-porter. He sensed him rather than recognizing him, for the man was no longer burdened or bent over but upright and sturdy, his shoulders reminiscent of a block of stone, his face mute and his eyes innocent: a statue of flesh.

The man with the round eyes advanced toward him.

"You're a porter?"

"Yes, Monsieur."

"Are you busy this evening?"

"I've just finished work."

"Would you like to earn some extra money?"

"Yes."

"Follow me."

He stayed in the shadows for the sake of prudence, although the disappearance of a street-porter is not the sort of thing that attracts a lot of attention.

When the man followed him, a newcomer—the theater critic that we saw in the first chapter—happened to be behind them. He had aged; the Julius affair, in which he had played a minor role, had closed many doors to him. His hair had gone prematurely gray.

The doors behind which there was anything improper and those of imbeciles had been closed to him since Julius' trial. It is necessary to put on a show of honesty, a veneer of honesty; those doors are the most carefully varnished and their owners are aware of its fragility; everything dirties them.

"The work I mentioned to you is outside Paris," the man with the round eyes said to the porter, who made no reply. "It's a matter of carrying delicate items of furniture from one floor to another. One strong individual is better for that than several. You seemed suitable."

"I am strong, in fact, and don't often break things." His voice was so calm that the man with the round eyes shivered.

From the end of the street, the critic didn't lose sight of them. Behind them, he took a cab,

"Twenty francs to follow that carriage," he said to the coachman. "I don't know how far it's going, but that's all I have. If you need more, I'll give you an IOU."

"It's enough," said the coachman, smacking his lips. Not having noticed who had got into the other fiacre, he thought it was an amorous matter.

"Follow at a distance," said the young man, "So that no one notices."

"Perhaps the father or the husband is with the lady, eh?"

"That's it, exactly."

The perspicacious coachman put a great deal of skill into following the designated vehicle, and it was not his fault that, when the carriage stopped in the middle of the Rue Vieille-du-Temple, the two men who got out of it disappeared into a house where no light was shining.

Any hope of finding them again was lost, for that could not be where they were going. It was ridiculous to have taken a cab to travel a few hundred yards, after having covered twice that distance so briskly in order to catch it.

"Well," said the coachman, "that wasn't worth the trouble of whipping the old nag! Anyway, she's not there, your beauty. The father's simply going off somewhere with a comrade; their nags must be inside."

The young man became anxious. "Wait," he said.

They waited—but no one came out.

Suddenly, the critic noticed the simplest thing in the world; the carriage had moved off, silently.

Damn! he thought, deciding to take a risk. "Hey, Citizen Coachman, who see things so well, have you noticed that the fiacre is no longer there?"

"Holy thunder! You're right."

He went back to the rank, not expecting to find the cab-driver. He was there, though. He had been paid when his passengers got out, not by the worker but the gentleman; he had put the price of the journey into his hand without saying anything; his horse was tired; he hadn't asked anything more; he lived nearby; he had come back.

It was because the man with the round eyes, having observed that they were being followed, had acted accordingly.

"We're going in here," he had said to his companion.

They had gone in without any objection from the porter. The house had a back door, of which he sometimes made use; he asked his companion to pick up a few objects from a lady's apartment and led him along a corridor to the other exit, somewhat surprised by the worker's silence.

"What do you think this house is?"

"I don't think anything; it's not my business."

"I'll explain if you wish."

"No need. Is it here that it's necessary to transport the furniture?"

"You're not there; we're going to take another cab; I didn't keep the first because the horse was poor."

"It doesn't matter." That tranquil tone sent shivers through the flesh of the man with the round eyes; it was necessary to finish with this diabolical porter.

The placid workman thought that he was strong, that he had a good six-shot revolver in his pocket, and that he was about to solve the mystery that had doomed Julius.

The critic had not given up either, in spite of the unfortunate way that his cab-chase had turned out.

"You see like a good chap to me," he said to the coachman. "It's not a matter of losing a woman but saving a man. Do you know which street runs behind the Rue du Temple? The house into which the two men went must have another door. Do you know where?"

He reflected briefly. "It's the Rue Thorigny, opening on the Rue Saint-Claude."

"Let's go."

This time, the perspicacious coachman was not mistaken; he knew his Paris. They did indeed find the entrance to the Rue Thorigny on the Rue Saint-Claude, leading in the exact direction of the suspect house. The street was as deserted as could be, apart from a girl walking her "beat" fervently, dying of hunger and fatigue. It was the black-haired La Boulotte,[23] acquitted because she had blamed everything on Frauchen and Rosen, who had got ten years, in spite of the fact that the kid wasn't dead—as La Boulotte knew better than anyone.

She recognized the critic, who was exploring the street with his new friend. There was nothing unusual about it.

"Where's the nearest cab-stand."

"This way, I think."

"Hey," said La Boulotte, "perhaps what you're looking for isn't far away. You won't find better, I'm telling you. It'll make up a bit for the dirty swine who just cheated me, treating me like a chamber-pot, you know?"

---

[23] The term *boulotte* [fat] has previously been used as a trivial noun with respect to this character, but it is capitalized here and deployed as if it were a nickname.

She followed them, keeping up her patter. "No reply, eh? I know you—you, the fat one, and you too, Long-legs. Have you changed your name since your mate's trial? Is it Marcellus now, you fat pig? Come on—it's not worth the trouble of climbing back into your rattletrap; the thing's gone bad."

As they did not reply, think of seeking information at the nearest cab-stand, La Boulotte began to howl, which brought out a dozen ragged-trousered rogues in flat caps. In the dawn light that was beginning to gleam, there was a brawl, all the more furious because Marcellus and the cab-driver, wanting to get past at any cost, lashed out, one using his whip to sting the assailants in the face, the other whirling his cane like a windmill; he knew how to use a Breton pen.

They didn't get far; a swarm of agents intervened. Marcellus, the coachman, the horse and the carriage were taken the police station, and as they were covered in blood from the blows they had received, that proved what the rogues and the whore said. That was why Marcellus and the cab-driver were sent to the lock-up for having been attacked. The man with the round eyes and the porter got away.

This time it really was toward the Bièvre that he took his companion.

A villa in the rustic style, where tree-branches extended over surrounding walls of medium height; a villa without suspicion, since it didn't even have a concierge—such was the peaceful nest of the man with the round eyes. In truth, like all prudent beasts, he had several holes.

Having introduced the porter into the first room, he turned up the wick of an enormous lamp that was waiting for him, lowered like a night-light.

"I'm so peaceful," he said, "that I prefer to remain alone. Perhaps that surprises you?"

"I just do my work. Where, if you please, are the objects to transport?"

The man with the round eyes sensed that he was going about things the wrong way with his explanations; he shivered, but his companion did not seem to notice. He was definitely afraid of this street-porter.

"Sit down. I want you to have a drink before getting to work."

"As you wish."

Still as impassive, the porter sat down stiffly; one might have thought him a man of stone, so solid did he seem.

When the two glasses were full of bronze-colored wine, the boss—who was not proud—clinked glasses with his worker. The porter, suddenly seeming anxious, said: "Listen, don't say anything. There's someone under that window—one might think that a mob were gathering."

Going pale, the man with the round eyes ran to the indicated place. When he came back, the glasses had been switched.

"There's nothing there!"

"Possibly. One would think, nevertheless, that there were people. One might even think that they ran away when you went toward them. Perhaps the gate is still open."

The gate, still open? The man with the round eyes knew that that was impossible, unless the accursed porter had opened it again—but no, he had been walking ahead of him.

It was not an occasion for trembling, but for action.

"Your health, comrade!"

The two men emptied their glasses.

"It's good wine, isn't it?"

"Very good."

"In a minute, I'll show you what needs to be done."

But now the man with the round eyes stands up, turns round, and falls like a dead weight. You'll recall that the glasses had been switched.

The porter picks him up, deposits him to a chaise-longue, and—in case he is only asleep—ties him up with curtains whose dimensions are too convenient for them not to have been used for that purpose before. Then he gets ready to explore the house. After his working clothes—which conceal a second costume, simple and commonplace, in black cloth—have been thrown into the fireplace, his long blond hair goes the same way; he is unrecognizable with his short-cropped black hair and black garments.

This transformation accomplished, Yves Kergaël took a candle from the candelabrum, set fire to the discarded garments, and looked around while they were burning. Then he checked on the man with the round eyes—who wasn't dead.

Yves took the sleeper's keys and opened the cupboard from which the wine had come; it was filled with phials that left no doubt as to their nature, along with a few bottles of delicate wines.

Neither the wines not the phials bore any label, of course, except the innocent word *déposé*.[24]

As he opened a door in that first room, something enormous bounded toward him, to the full extent of its chain. It was one of those Gallic mastiffs whose final

---

[24] "Laid down"—which is commonly used with respect to wine, but carries obvious double meanings.

representatives, after certain butcheries at the Barrière du Combat, had disappeared in the face of public indignation—which had, as always, blamed the dogs rather than their masters. Dogs are hardly responsible for the training they receive.

The mastiff must have been hidden, since its breed was banned; it would have been dangerous for the beast to go out into the street. That was perfectly simple; it's permissible to love one's dog. What appeared less straightforward to Kerdrel[25] was the way in which the enormous carnivore had been placed close to the place where its master put to sleep those who had inconvenienced him while awake. One never puts people to sleep without having an idea of what to do next.

In the redoubt occupied by the beast, large as it was, there was an unbearable charnel-house odor—but after all, animals don't use perfume. The porter didn't want to base a conclusion on that.

The dog had devoured its daily pittance, and that pittance was raw flesh; large bloody stains were visible around it.

"Lie down, Boull!" said the porter, using the name of its race at hazard.[26]

---

[25] This transformation of the surname links the character to his previous pseudonymous manifestation; the first name will also undergo a transformation shortly, although it will not quite revert to its previous form; that is probably accidental, but I have refrained from altering it in case it is deliberate.

[26] Although *dogue* [mastiff] is being used rather vaguely with respect to this fighting-dog, the clear implication is that it is somewhat larger than a bulldog or what we would nowadays call a "pit-bull" terrier, although the nickname would imply a breed of that sort to an English reader. It is probably more closely akin to a rottweiler.

The beast retreated and obeyed; Yves had guessed right. Everyone knows the effect produced on a dog by its name, spoken with a command or a caress; it usually does what it is told.

Yves Kerdrel carried the candle around the room; the charnel-house was real. It is permissible for a dog to have a bone-pile; it is even a right—but it is less so when one finds a child's finger therein, circled by a dainty ring with a false pearl—a jewel having no other value than a little girl's whim.

Still calm, Yves Kerdrel picked up the sinister debris and went through the rest of the house; it was innocent and tidy. The man with the round eyes was not imprudent enough to leave papers lying around or to have padded rooms. His dog was sufficient to dispose of the remains of his monstrous whims, and in order to satisfy them, the victim was immobilized in the same way that one immobilizes an animal whose dolorous movements might disturb the delicate tissues of its flesh during vivisection—she would suffer as usual, but could neither move nor cry out.

Yves explored the house from the cellars to the loft, but there was perfect innocence everywhere. Even the library only contained scholarly books on history, medicine and chemistry—which explained the phials. There was a dissecting table in a study completely surrounded by bookshelves; atlases of comparative anatomy were laid out on a side-table with scalpels.

Three or four guinea-pigs were roaming around the floor, awaiting their fate.

Every scientist belonging to the category of "intellectuals" has the right to have laboratories in which he dissects and vivisects anything he wishes, except for human animals; one can do anything one wants to animals.

Briefly, Yvan wondered whether he might really be in the home of a scholar, whether his host's unconsciousness might be natural, and the dog might have carried away the hand of a cadaver purchased for the laboratory.

He went back into the first room and examined the cupboard again.

A ledger placed on the first shelf recorded the results of experiments carried out on rabbits and guinea-pigs; evidently, if there was a search, the law would have no objection to raise, but there was too much precaution in putting the manuscript and the phials together like that, and the word *déposé* was equivalent to the "it wasn't me, guv," of every guilty street-urchin. Why was all this not in the laboratory? It wasn't rabbits and guinea-pigs that were put to sleep here, in order to transport them there afterwards.

The dog pulled at its chain, uttering vague sighs. Yvan realized that the beast was mute. Ordinarily, one does not carry out operations of that sort on guard-dogs. The dog had evidently been subjected to precautions, for an apparatus placed on its muzzle must have robbed it of its sense of smell.

Yvan passed the candle in front of the dog's eyes. It was blind. Only hearing remained to it; perhaps its master had left it that in order that it would not devour itself.

The Bièvre only got a few bones when the dog had done its work; then again, there were other means of making gnawed skulls and other debris disappear; museums of anthropology received some of them, aged by procedures known to the man with the round eyes and labeled: skulls of Egyptians, Slavs, etc, according to their form.

Yvan thought that if the dog had been treated in this way, it was because if it had been allowed to know what work it was doing, it would have refused. Elephants only kill by virtue of being trained and intoxicated. This beast was the same.

"Here, Boull!" said Yvan, moving closer to the dog, which lay down at his feet, weary of not being stroked—or, perhaps, in its instinctive honesty, weary of belonging to a monster; beasts do these things, which cannot be explained

Yvan undid the apparatus placed over the poor animal's nostrils, which maintained odors capable of blocking the most subtle sense of smell. This time, the animal was conquered.

Poor creature! Yvan said to himself. *I don't want to leave you here; you'll be very inconvenient, but no matter! And who knows, perhaps you'll be the best possible assistant?* He released the dog, which bounded into the next room, stopped in front of the divan and leapt backwards on scenting its master.

It was definitely there that it had often been given its pittance; this time, with the apparatus removed, it was afraid.

That was the only sign of attention it gave its former master—or, at least, Yvan did not give it time for more. Having put a carafe of fresh water on the table next to the wretch, he left him to the heavy sleep from which he would wake up with the alarm of a spider caught in its own web.

Sniffing the fresh air outside, the dog threw itself so violently upon Yvan to caress him that it almost knocked him over; there were tears in the martyrized beast's extinct eyes.

No more was heard of the adventures of the man with the round eyes; a trifle pale, he set out the next morning to liquidate the assets he possessed under various names, and left for a long voyage.

The notary who bought for himself, at a price too low to mention, the house we have just seen, found absolutely nothing remarkable there. The phials no longer existed, the laboratory no longer contained either the dissecting-tale or any manuscripts—but what astonished the notary was that a fire had taken hold—he could not tell how—in the floorboards of a room adjacent to the first room, but had been extinguished on the threshold. That was strange—but the main thing was that the damage was not considerable.

The critic and the cab-driver got away with a fortnight in prison, but it became impossible for them to find employment. Wasn't one a recidivist, and the other the friend of a recidivist? Don't forget that, even though one has not been convicted at a first trial, one is still a recidivist in the minds of the credulous. They left together for America.

Neither the street-porter nor the dog was ever seen again. It's true that a blacksmith of Herculean strength had just moved into one of the poorest streets in La Villette, with a big dog with fur as thick as a bear's, who made the bellows of his smithy roar.

Julius is almost rehabilitated, the blacksmith thought.

He was mistaken, for he could not pick up the trail of the man with the round eyes, and it would have been necessary to leave France for the second part of the mission that he and Olaff had undertaken.

XI. At the South Pole[27]

Fringes of flame in the black sky; it is the austral polar aurora quivering in the air like red crêpe. The silence of the desert! Semi-submerged beneath the marine prairies through which the English brig *Whale*, commanded by Captain Josiah, was searching for a bay in order to get as close as possible to the snow-covered land, enormous unknown monsters came to see the brig at close range.

The *Whale*'s crew was not numerous, but they were hardy sea-dogs. There was only one passenger, Olaff, but he was not an ordinary passenger; he could put his hands to work as well as, if not better than, the most audacious of the whalers. It was for his stirring audacity as much as his knowledge that Josiah had brought him.

It's necessary for men, like racehorses, dogs and every other animal, to be trained, Josiah thought, *and a trainer who works on himself is precious.*

He knew, moreover, that the regions where the cold is most intense are known and that the pole must be reachable; during his whaling expeditions he had reached many lands in the southern hemisphere whose existence is unsuspected, and none of those that have been discovered were unknown to him.

At about eighty degrees of latitude he had recognized volcanic mountains four or five thousand meters

---

[27] This section of the narrative must surely have been transplanted from an early work—apparently a Vernian romance—and it remains quite irrelevant to the main narrative until the latter reaches its epilogue, when it helps set up the sequel.

high and, like James Ross,[28] he believed that the pole could be reached overland.

With his sailors—hewn out of bocks of granite he said, for such enterprises—he would doubtless have reached the objective of his adventure, but none of them was able to help him with anything other than bodily strength. Perhaps he had wanted it thus; Josiah was a cold calculator, a cold explorer, a cold scholar; he wanted to make his voyage comfortable in all respects, and especially to obtain a profit from it. Another scholar would have been an embarrassment if he had wanted to sacrifice the productive part of the venture to the exploratory part. That was why, for many years. He had waited patiently until he encountered the man he needed, a man whose audacity was proof against anything, who, moved by some passion, even went beyond the goal.

That was the main thing, but it was not necessary that the man should amuse himself debating various points of the voyage of which he was certain. The scholar he took with him must neither debate nor recoil, must go straight ahead, must serve in good faith as the expedition's trainer; if necessary, he would end him forth with part of the crew, while he went forth with the other, and unless death intervened, they would meet up at the requisite point. Josiah thought that in certain circumstances, one does not have the time to die; when he saw Olaff for the first time, the latter said a few words to him that were a revelation.

---

[28] James Ross led the most significant Antarctic expedition of the early nineteenth century, between 1839 and 1843, succeeding in mapping the coastline of the polar continent

Josiah had his man! It was in Rose Street,[29] at an evening meeting at which German, French and English socialists were assembled.

"Two things are required," Olaff said. "The right time and worldly wealth. With those two things, liberty will rise over the entire world!"

On going out, Olaff felt a tap on his shoulder. His face was not exactly friendly when he saw the bulky gentleman, six feet tall and as stiff as a hop-pole, who had permitted himself that familiarity.

That expression leased Josiah. *There's a energetic man*, he said to himself.

After five minutes' conversation, everything was settled.

"You need a vast fortune?" Josiah had said. "Do you want one?"

At first Olaff thought he was dealing with a madman, but he was too good a physiognomist to retain that suspicion for long. "Yes," he said. "I want one."

"You might not like the means of acquiring it?"

"I only ask that they be certain."

"They're infallible, if we survive—and we will survive—the voyage."

"It's the voyage of which I've dreamed, then?"

"It is indeed; perhaps such affinities are explicable."

Josiah's conditions filled eight compactly-written pages. No article was contrary to Olaff's principles. He signed, and it was agreed that Josiah would notify him

---

[29] Rose Street was by no means as respectable in the 1880s as it is today, although the Lamb and Flag, reputedly the oldest pub in London, is still there, its owners still proud of the fact that it back room was once known as "the Bucket of Blood."

138

immediately before departure—which, as the reader knows, he did.

To depart in a brig to traverse the Atlantic as far as the Antarctic circle, it would require Josiah to expect to get there, much less to get back again. He had already made the voyage five times; his brig belonged to him; he loved it as if he had animated it—coldly, though, as Josiah was able to love.

The brig was solidly built of Indian oak; iron and steel being armored by one another therein; its hull was enormously resistant.

With a certain satisfaction, Josiah showed Olaff the quantities of supplies laid in for the voyage; there were condensed foodstuffs so nutritious in nature that a single grain provided the sustenance of a full meal; on previous voyages he had left enormous provisions to await him. One could not develop scurvy with his conserves, in which appropriate does were condensed of iron, the sugars of antiscorbutic plants, cinchona, etc.—a thousand things that ought to conserve and even augment, the strength of the crew and prevent illness.

The ship's doctor, completely in accord with Josiah's ides, claimed that human life, with preservatives and reparatives, could be prolonged far beyond its usual duration, and he hoped to prolong his own indefinitely, which would make it amenable to accommodating the changes produced by life in the native lands of the various human tribes.

In addition to the twenty crewmen, there were a dozen large English mastiffs aboard, intended to haul sleds, if necessary. They would almost always be fed on fish caught during the voyage. The sharks that took it into their heads to follow the ship did not usually follow it for long.

We have mentioned that Olaff had saved Josiah's life; this is how it came about:

One day, the captain, who counted and examined everything personally, after having checked that the men were in good health, from himself to the lowliest crew member, passed on to an inspection of the dogs. One of the largest grabbed Josiah's clothing unexpectedly; taken by surprise, he fell so awkwardly that one of his feet caught in the rigging. The dog's foaming maw was already on his face when the beast collapsed, felled by a crow-bar wielded by Olaff.

"Thanks," said Josiah. "Even if the animal had been rabid, with a good cupping-glass applied to the wound, I'd have got away with it—it's not the first time—but it would have devoured my face, and it was such a large dog that I'd have been disfigured." He passed his hand over his face, caressing his cheeks.

Josiah was vain enough to think that he was handsome, so people claimed—but perhaps they said it in order to find a weakness in him. At any rate, if he thought that he was handsome he was wrong.

Before anchoring, Josiah assembled his crew and, although he did not usually say much, made a long speech.

"My friends, each of us has a project to which he sacrifices his life. Every project requires more wealth than you have, for this is your first voyage. My first companions were three in number; they're now richer than English lords. Personally, I've made six voyages, which proves that one can come back. There are bandit chiefs who lead their men to prey upon other men, but I'm leading you to prey on nature, where no man has the courage or the means to go.

"Perhaps we'll be obliged to split up into three groups; in that case, the doctor and Olaff will each taken seven men, to whom I'll give orders to obey them as they would obey me. It's science that is in command here, it's necessary to save lives; they have science and you only have courage; with the wealth that you'll have for your share, your sons will have both.

"Look through this veil of mist, beyond these marine prairies full of enormous monsters, at the midnight sun gleaming out there and the ice-peaks like diamonds, Isn't all that beautiful? And look, through the curtain of mist, do you see those immense ears of corn standing out like red sheaves in the sky—that's the aurora australis. Isn't it true that it's a fine spectacle?

"Let's go, then—forward march! And never lose sight, until further orders, of the peak directly ahead of us, which looms over all the rest; it's at the foot of that peak that we'll find out whether the expedition is to split up; we'll go that far on the first stage."

"Hurrah!" shouted the sailors. "Hurrah for England!"

They only named old Albion out of habit, for deep down, those men—whose families, for the most part, were dying of starvation—scarcely thought about their nationality. Poverty is universal.

They were thinking that when they returned, their aged mothers and their young daughters would have their bread assured, if their aged mothers had not died and the young girls had not been sold fresh to old ogres.

While the dogs were harnessed in order to carry packs, if necessary, or pull sleds, and their health was being checked, each man filled his game-bag, from which we would never be separated, with tablets of condensed nourishment, ammunition for their rifles, etc., under the supervision of the doctor. Josiah, while checking everything, took Olaff to one side.

"I won't ask you," he said, "to keep the secret with regard to your companions back home; it's obvious that you're only going to the discovery with the objective that you mentioned in Rose Street, for which you need worldly wealth. But I want your word not to make the mines you're going to see the official objective of a governmental expedition."

Olaff cut Josiah off with a laugh that reassured him; he could be tranquil. The entire world could have exploited the mines that Olaff was about to see without exhausting them for a long time, but any monopoly would have rendered them useless for everyone except for the band of explorers who had raced there.

The brig was anchored to a rock that Josiah knew. "It's reliable," he said. "I've entrusted the *Whale* to it three times, and three launches. The men and dogs began climbing the steep slope of a mound that had to be the polar continent, one shore of which is named Adelie Land and the other Clarie Land.

Flocks of albatrosses, like doves, filled the horizon on which the aurora australis was shaking the polar cupola on high, like a winnowing-basket, with its thousand of flamboyant ears of corn.

XI. The Brig

You will remember from Josiah's roll-call[30] Moses, Lazarus, Olivier, Vill and Walter. In the same order in which they had been named, the five men walked silently, following Doctor Daniel.

From time to time, the physician turned his head and looked at the peak at the foot of which the crevasse extended. He was making sure of the direction of their return.

The tempest howled with increasing strength; the sea battered the breaches in the snowy projections; the shore stood out white against the black waves, creating the illusion beneath the thick mist of an immense sheet quivering in the darkness—perhaps the white shroud of the dead.

They advanced slowly through the snow. About half way, Daniel shouted: "Halt!" He wanted to stoke up the human machines with fuel.

Each of them took a few tablets of conserves out of his back, swallowed them silently, and resumed walking.

An hour later, they arrived on the shore, but the launches had been torn away from the cove in which they had been anchored. That cove, of which Josiah had

---

[30] This is the most obvious point in the narrative where text definitely appears to be missing; an entire chapter, at least, appears to have been mislaid, during which the roll-call the reader is presumed to remember must have taken place, along with the accident with regard to which this chapter's rescue mission has been launched.

made use without mishap in three expeditions, had just been violated by the tempest.

No more launches! The men stopped, in despair. Out there, people were waiting, on behalf of the seven men who had been swallowed up.

"There are three more launches on the brig," said Daniel. "We'll bring back two, to make sure."

Bring them back! That was all very well-but it was necessary to get to them first.

They were not left in uncertainty for long.

All the *Whale*'s seamen were good swimmers; all of them, too, by virtue of a precaution that Josiah, or perhaps Daniel, had ordered them to take, were wearing supple double-ply one-piece vestments that covered their bodies from the neck to the knees, and the arms from the shoulder to the wrist. They did not inhibit movement, and permitted them to carry that sole garment for all eventualities.

He ordered two of them to take off these vestments, which each of them put into a well-sealed oilskin and suspended around his neck. He did the same.

"We'll dry off on the brig," he said, "and when we put them back on, we'll be warm."

Another "fuel-tablet," as he called them, was swallowed. Then, pointing at a white dot that was dancing on the waves—Josiah painted the hulls of his ships in that color—he said: "To the brig!"

The four men, their eyes fixed on the white dot, launched themselves into the mist where snow was floating over the waves.

I don't know whether anyone has ever attributed to the Devil, to whom so many things are attributed, a more extraordinary feat of swimming, especially accomplished without mishap. All four of them reached the ship; two fell down, overcome by fatigue and cold when they arrived on deck.

"Come on!" said Daniel. "Friction, put on the vests, a little rum, and get going!"

They had no need of encouragement, the brave men, but the doctor's serenity pleased them.

The two launches, towed by a minuscule steam-launch, were set afloat. It was the launches that took up most room on the *Whale*.

In spite of the gusts of wind, the men who had stayed on the shore had built a fire, which served as a beacon for the launches.

How the steersman contrived to get them there, Daniel himself could only ever comprehend by means of the words: He had to!

The three launches were dragged on to the shore and wedged in a hollow in the rocks. All that work had taken the handful of men nearly eight hours. It was necessary to substitute for numbers by means of feats of strength worthy of the cleverest circus-performers.

None of the members of the expedition had perished, but back there the ground had split, isolating Josiah and his men as if on an island. The cracks surrounding them were broadening, but it was necessary to await the return of the expedition. What could have become of the unfortunates who had been buried?

The whiteness of the snow and the double red fringe of the aurora australis brightened the sad scene, lending it a desolate grandeur.

The snow on the summits was coming down again, driven by the wind over the slopes and dissolving into foam over the waves.

The wind had doubled, as sailors say. In the midst of all that, the expedition arrived.

"I've brought the steam engine and two launches," said Daniel.

"I thought so," Josiah replied.

He also thought that the ship might well sink, and was already seeking a means of substituting for it, whether by making a tour of the austral continent on foot and setting off for North America in launches, or by constructing an aerostat, all the materials for which he had stored in a cave long ago. In the meantime, Josiah was having roped tied under his arms in order descend into the crevasse when, with a noise like the detonation of a thousand cannon, an enormous piece of ice detached itself from the bank.

Heavily, the block started moving back and forth in the tempest like a raft, with gleams of green-tinted gems beneath the livid aurora.

From beneath the ice-raft, which was the size of a hill, the waves projected an enormous jet of water over the men grouped around Josiah.

Human forms, vague in the uncertain light, were floating on the waves brought closer by the indentation of the sea. It had bitten into the shore furiously, as deeply as the foot of the mountain. Those human forms were drowned men; they could be counted. Only Olaff was missing.

The waves, engulfed in the caverns of ice, had brought back the corpses.

"Let's go, Captain, let's go!" The men, standing up, seemed to have forgotten all the fatigues of the journey. They were pointing toward the interior of the valley.

Daniel stood there, waiting.

"Fix that rope solidly," said Josiah, without paying any heed to the urgency of his men to flee the ground undermined by the waves, battered by the winds and torn apart by the assault of the elements.

"Pull me up at five-minute intervals," Josiah continued. "It's obvious that Olaff hasn't stayed in the same place. I'll go down every side of the crevasse. I've never abandoned a single companion without knowing his fate."

"Hurrah for the captain!" His matelots were ready for anything now.

But Josiah did not have time to make his descent.

A second crack, more frightful than the first, separated their islet of ice completely; it took on an oscillatory movement, then settled, drawing away like a raft.

Men were accumulated on the ice-wreck, fourteen in number, with nine dogs. The tenth howled with a quasi-human voice watching the others, from which it had been separated, move away.

"Poor Fet," said Josiah, and then quickly resumed is usual impassivity. He went on: "We have no need to fear famine; each of us is carrying provisions for a long time; as for the dogs that remain, the sea will provide for their needs until the waves throw us into a cove; we're going to follow the coast between the groups of islands and the continent." As if talking to himself, he added: "No one has made a considerable number of voyages without disaster; one had to happen sooner or later."

Those who were making their first voyage would have much preferred that it had not happened this time, but Daniel calmness did them good, and they were brave men; finally, they imagined—without being much mistaken—that this sort of thing always happened, at least once, to everyone, as Josiah said.

"If we survive," Daniel said, "there's every assurance for the remainder of the expedition. It's rare to encounter such geological turbulence, and these collapses have the good side of showing new things to those who survive them."

Through the tempest they could distinguish the flight of black clouds, like birds' wings beating the horizon; and then everything—the tempest in the sky and the tempest of the waves—became confused in profound darkness. The raft drifted aimlessly; two or three dogs slipped into the sea.

When a calm came, the castaways saw, drifting like them, a fragment of the ice-sheet to which the Whale was attached, dancing at the end of its cable like a cockchafer at the end of a piece of thread. It was the block of ice to which the anchor had been attached.

"Listen," said Josiah. "This has happened to me before. If fate brings us closer to the brig, we'll swim to it; if it's not too far away, we'll attempt that chance of salvation. I hardly think we'll get two chances—we have to grab this one."

Josiah's slightly fantastic hope was justified, thanks to the wildness of the tempest, which gripped the ice-floes in a gyratory movement, spun them around, and caused them to collide with one another, alternately drawn them apart and together.

It was a marvel that the ship wasn't smashed; that was because of the slack given to it by its cable—but it was inevitable that the anchor-chain would break if the tempest did not die down soon.

The men were ready to try to board her.; it seemed less terrible than staying where they were. As in oceanic cyclones, an immense calm succeeded the fury of the elements. Placidly, at the tip of a cluster of ice-floes like floating islets, the *Whale* was still there.

"All right!" said Josiah, diving into the sea.

Men and dogs followed him. As if by a miracle, they found ropes attached to the bulwarks.

There's someone on the brig, Josiah and Daniel thought.

Without those ropes, the exhausted men would only have reached their goal with a supreme effort of will, and the dogs would have been left behind. Three of them remained—the leaders of each harness-team. Doubtless more intelligent, they had stayed in the middle of the floe, trampled by the feet and bruised by the weight of the men; they had sensed that they ought not to leave the place where they were being crushed. They were hauled on board.

A man standing on the deck welcomed his companions; it was Olaff. The sea had dragged him from the tunnel he had been exploring all the way to the rock to which the brig was still attached. A few minutes later, the ice-sheet had broken away.

The men uttered a cry of fright, thinking he must be a ghost.

"Very good!" said Josiah, with no other demonstration, exactly as if he had left Olaff a few moments before. "You did well to lower the ropes."

Thus, Josiah had no need of the aerostat of which he had dreamed; the *Whale* only had broken masts. The passes they had gone through and the wealth they had discovered would be used to accomplish Olaff's dream, for they would be able to return.

Winds change and fortune is capricious, though, and Josiah's sentiment was opposed by one final catastrophe.

He had been right until then, as Dr. Daniel delighted in repeating, increasingly persuaded that what two, or even three of them had now accomplished ought to be attributed to Josiah alone. He would have attributed the creation of the universe to him, had he not been increasingly certain of its environmental transformations through the ages.

Josiah, then, had accomplished the voyage thanks, above all, to the courage of the fifteen surviving men, and even that of the dogs who, as a reward, were brought back to lead an easy life in the home of the cook, who had claimed them, having neither parents, nor a wife, nor children with who to share his portion of the wealth. With them, he said, he wouldn't be alone.

The dislocations of the ground had brought to light forests buried in primitive eras; the crew had to shortage of fuel.

By virtue of an accident with a lamp they set fire to one of these coal-mines, which was still burning and would burn for a long time, but no one had died. The subterranean heat propagated by the fire had even been useful to them. Mines of sulfur, gold and diamonds, not only known to Josiah but brought to light by the recent quakes, had permitted them to load the ship, but not to the point of imprudence.

"It's not much," said Olaff, who had demonstrated a frightful severity in the search, "but it's enough to buy arms; perhaps, if we have to fight tomorrow, it wouldn't come out badly."

Gazing into space, he looked beyond the terrible struggle to the days of the great peace in which human progress would march into light and liberty—and from his eyes, which no longer shed tears, a moist dew fell.

A few of the sailors—I don't know how—had partially penetrated his secret; one of them came to him one day, sent by the others.

"Comrade Olaff," he said, "We know what you want to do, and we've come to offer to do our part. We'll come back."

Olaff simply extended his arms to the mariner; he accepted. "We'll come back together," he said, "if I'm still alive."

Two men standing behind him witnessed that scene. As always, it was Josiah who spoke.

"Everything on the ship," he said, "belongs to what you want to do. Don't thank me; I believe that science will gain from it—and then again, I'm curious to see the upheaval. It isn't written, in any case, that old Albion will remain tranquil; I've seen many birds raise their chicks in fallen trees, far from the trunk cut for the fire; but in the next generation, all the human nestlings will fly together toward the new shore.

"As for the voyage, we'll all come back, I believe."

Josiah was mistaken, for he never saw anyone again.

Not far from the channel at Brest, the *Whale* went down, either because a breach had pence in her hull or because she had suddenly taken on water.

One dog, an excellent swimmer, came ashore exhausted, and died on the strand. Around its neck was a tin-plate box containing an account of the voyage addressed by Olaff to his friend. A few lines had been added in pencil:

The brig's sinking; it's taking on water without our being able to discover how. We'll take to the launches. If I perish, let someone else remake the voyage that you know. One bee is nothing in the hive. Note he is a good swimmer; I'll entrust this to him.

They had, indeed, taken to the launches and had loaded them with a fraction of the wealth; that took time;

the pumps were ineffective against the water invading he hold.

In the beautiful wood of the isles, well-protected between successive patched repairs, unknown legions of rats had been swarming for years; they hull had been pierced. Just as the men were about to climb into the launches the Whale, with a horrible splintering sound, sank beneath the waves from which nothing rises again.

The friend left behind by Olaff had accomplished half of the giant task that they had shared; he knew that the returning brig was sailing for France instead of London.

At the first royal crime—they were not rare—the soil of the despotisms would have been strewn with the dead leaves of centuries of winters.

And now the shipwreck had occurred.

Russia had been waiting for Olaff's dispatch; the dispatch had come; the signal had been doubly given by acts of despotism. The new Europe had risen from the soil, and now it was all sunk in the Ocean. All his zeal would now seem quixotic; he had not succeeded; there would be ridicule, and that would put a stain on the Revolution, everything he loved.

Who knows what will surge forth, he thought, *when they know that I know that I didn't want to survive? Olaff was right; others will remake the voyage whose audacity demands success; one bee less is nothing in the hive; it doesn't inhibit the honey.*

The Herculean blacksmith, a long time absent from his poor house in Belleville, had only been back there for a few days when his neighbors became alarmed at no longer seeing him pass by, or the big blind dog that was so well able to follow him along the sidewalk to the newspaper-stall.

Rumor had been heard of epidemics, and it was not good to leave corpses unburied, especially in such times as those. Thanks to the terror of microbes, the blacksmith's door was opened.

They were both asleep forever, the dog killed in such a way that it would not suffer, with a bullet in the ear, the man more harshly: he had put the barrel of the revolver in his mouth, and the debris of his brain had splashed the walls.

Why would he have left his blind companion behind in order that it might be unhappy? To give his own life was good; to take that of another for the same cause was understandable; as long as the heart beats in the breast, one is repelled by needless cruelties; it would have been coldly cruel to abandon the poor beast. Everything that suffers and dies, and suffers from your absence, should not be left behind; it is necessary not to abandon a heart as one leaves an object.

XIII. The Lost Children

They had to move fast, the people who were searching for little Ellen; they were not moving fast enough.

Then again, it's so difficult to find a child lost in the world.

Those who were searching for her did not include her mother, who believed her dead, nor her father; it was Doctor Gaël, with the aid of Madame Basis—who obeyed him out of religious dread, as she would have obeyed the Devil or the good Lord.

To make sure that he would not catch cold, and out of jealousy of his colleague the alienist, who had delivered him asleep, when Jabouille awoke, he said to him: "It's necessary to put you to sleep, imbecile, in order that we can have a chat."

Jabouille's state of mind can be imagined. Terrified, he made no reply.

"Come on, animal, I won't do you any harm; that would be quite useless to science—and anyway, I have need of you. Can you listen to me and understand me?"

Jabouille, trembling all over, tried to nod his head.

"Listen: you've been an agent; I'm going to send you in quest of a lost child; you have to find her for me."

"Where is she, Monsieur?"

"If I knew, I wouldn't need you. Her name's Ellen; she's black-haired; she's been lost for two years. She was ten then, so she must be about twelve, perhaps thirteen. If you can find her, you won't have to leave me again."

By Jabouille's grimace, the doctor saw that he had taken the wrong tack with that promise.

"All right, imbecile, I'll give you whatever you want."

"But who will let me carry out my search, Monsieur? I'll be taken for a conspirator."

The doctor reflected. "You seem very stupid," he said, "but even so, people might contrive to make that mistake. Listen; I'll give you a means: you can pass yourself off as a member of the secret police, and it won't be a lie. I'm appointing you head of my secret police of science; it's to me that you'll give all the information you acquire, marked with appropriate signs. This seal bears the first and last letter of the Indian alphabet, known as *daiwandgari*, the writing of the divine city. If anyone asks you where these lines come from, you'll reply that you've sworn never to reveal it, and, moreover, you'll swear to me that you'll simply say: 'The master knows that that means.'

"You'll keep away from any meeting that has a scientific, political or even literary character; you'd be interrogated and answer stupidly. With that precaution, you'll never be arrested. Here, in writing, is the incomplete information that we have. Sniff out the trail and follow it. Instinct is strongly developed in you. You know how to hide; you'll discover how the child must be hidden. She was stolen in Spain; that's the only place she can't be. The little girl about twelve years old whose disappearance was reported a few months ago might well be her, but it would be extraordinary to find her so quickly. See the slut who was acquitted, though—she's the one who ought to know where the child is.

"This is why you ought to be able to find the child: it's because the necessity of hiding yourself has left traces throughout your organism that will serve you marvelously every time you want to find another hidden individual. There's also the suggestion, which I won't neglect, you can be sure; you'll obey me at a distance as at close range. Do you still know how to spell?"

"Not very well."

"So much the better! If you fall into some hornets' nest, it'll be easy for you to get out of it. You'll only be accused of being a minion, and you'll be kept alive in order to discover those behind you."

Jabouille dared not say that there was nothing reassuring about that prospect. He wondered why Gaël was not conducting his search officially.

The doctor replied to his thought. "When it's a matter of a lost pretty girl, the search must be carried out secretly to succeed; one might have to deal with a procuress of human flesh or an adoptive mother who has concentrated all her affection on the child, and neither one will talk. From the emperor of a heap of nations to a vagabond, everyone hides his prey in all usual cases. You'll address your letters to Madame Basis. She's the one to whom I'll dictate the replies. She'll employ her style and orthography. In case of extraordinary peril, address yourself to me and sign with the two letters of the daiwandgari. I shan't say any more for fear of putting you on a false trail. Go!"

Jabouille lowered his head and drew away. Something was weighing upon him. He did not even try to stop himself obeying.

Gradually, however, the affected instinct awoke groups of dormant sensations in Jabouille. His nerves vibrated in chords; his nervous fibers tautened, and the human harp, properly tuned, found a series of new faculties surging forth, like the sound of concentric circles. A transformation took place. It was not only in order to obey but with ardor that Jabouille searched for the little girl.

Search! Search! The primal instinct developed, one of the most ardent of the child and the beast.

Search! Search! And the young dog and the young human become animated, concentrating their faculties, searching, searching! Sometimes, the trail is hot; sometimes, they're far apart, but the ardor never lets up.

At first, it was hot, only to cool down thereafter.

Gaël was right; the fat black woman knew a great deal, but after that length, the thread suddenly snapped.

The best means of obtaining information from her was not to ask her for it.

Jabouille went one day to the Brasserie du Bel Escholier, of which she was an ornament, in spite of the jealousy of Angélique, who was no longer so much in fashion.

"Why, Monsieur Jabouille there you are! We haven't seen you for an eternity."

"I was by."

"Doing what? I thought you weren't at the prison anymore?"

"Ah," said Jabouille, evasively.

"Perhaps you got a job elsewhere?"

Jabouille remained silent.

"Perhaps you were up to something shady?"

"Something that worked up a thirst," said Jabouille.

"I've got just what you need—hang on."

She came back with a carafe of some diabolical liquor. *If he's doesn't spill everything in his belly with that*, she thought, *he'll burst.*

Jabouille poured himself a full glass, and a small one for La Boulotte, and kept pouring the small ones so frequently that when the brasserie closed he escorted La

Boulotte to her door. Drunk enough to puke, she had not lost sight of her obsessive desire to know Jabouille's secret, but it was her own she let slip.

"I have a desire," said Jabouille, "to take with me on my voyages the old woman with whom you were chatting one evening, Boulotte. She's not compromising and she knows a lot; I like to hear her talk."

That remark nearly sobered her up. She was frightened, and looked at Jabouille. He seemed to be as drunk as she was.

"Fetch La Maugrabine, and make her spill the beans! She never speaks a word of truth, and one can't go out with her; old as she is, she's always followed by some kid."

"That doesn't matter," said Jabouille. "I have the means of paying for a lady companion who *has connections*."

"As to that, there aren't many others who have *connections*."

"That's what I thought."

"Well, with that she-cat you won't get far—and it's necessary to find her."

"Oh, she was found a long time ago, and she had a lot to say about you, Boulotte."

"About me!" She started to tremble in spite of her drunkenness. "Whatever she can lay at my door, I know enough about hers."

It's said that the investigation's going to be reopened. I might be wrong, but I'm warming you. The little girl's been found; the old woman must have talked, she's been arrested—but she'll get out because she's revealed everything, and I'm going to take her away."

"What has she said about me, the old cadaver? I'm the one who'll tell what I know." That was imprudent, but La Boulotte was drunk.

The following morning, Jabouille knew that the old woman, who was English but was known as La Maugrabine because of her dark complexion,[31] had bought the child—whom she seemed to know—for the House of the Veiled Woman, whose bawd she was, precisely because the little girl had to disappear, but she kept running away. She had run away again, at the risk of being cut in two by railway carriages. La Boulotte knew that the old woman was actively searching for her, because the child was a danger to her.

These details, written in Jabouille's style, much more awkward on paper than when speaking, and with his spelling, were immediately addressed to Madame Basis for Dr. Gaël.

The thread broke there, and drifted in so many directions that it was difficult to pick it up again.

---

[31] This explanation implies that the term is being derived from an Arabic word referring to the inhabitants of Morocco and Spain, usually rendered Maghreb in English, but its Frenchification generates a similarity to *maugrer* [to grumble or to curse], also implying shrewishness.

XIV. The Brothel

Fog envelops London, as thickly as if the city were in the midst of a heap of ashes. The lights are on everywhere, as if it were night; it's scarcely midday.

Protected—or believing themselves to be—by the wall of a night-shelter, a pile of rags in lying pell-mell in the fog. They're vagabonds who arrived too late to get into the shelter.

The shelter, as full as an egg, could not contain a single person more; they could either wait until tomorrow to sleep or go to another shelter. They lacked the strength to go elsewhere, so they huddled against the wall and let the rain fall. Those underneath are warm, but they're choking. Those on top are soaked.

There are young and old, women and children.

The doors are opened; there are places vacant because some have gone out, their tasks completed. Some kinds of work are done therein, especially carding wool for mattresses; it's harsh work for the hardest hands, but vagabondage isn't punished by the courts.

Some have already gone in when a clamor erupts in the middle of the pile. There have been incidents.

A window carrying a baby in a sling around her neck and awaiting another not yet born, not having enough money to buy the roasted fish whose stink fills certain streets, has bought something to drink instead; it's cheaper. She had been moistened by that, and they don't know whether or not she's dead.

She's carried inside the shelter, the baby howling in its sling, suspended around the unfortunate woman's neck.

A young girl, pale and exhausted, her black hair soaked by the rain, her rags doubtless long since saturated with fog, looks at the door and dares not go in. Gripped by some hope, she drags herself along painfully, looking at the notices advertising for seamstresses. Poor thing!

She has stopped in front of one of those notices, and there is something that gives her courage, which steadies her on her feet, shod in horrible shoes stuffed with rags. She straightens up sand smoothes her hair. She doesn't know much English, but necessity sharpens her intelligence; she understands; she forces herself to understand.

Who knows whether she might be lucky enough to be accepted where young girls of her age are being solicited her easy and well-paid work?

Indeed, she was accepted, the poor thing, But easy and well-paid work does not exist for the proletariat anywhere beneath the heavens of the Old World..

The child was in a brothel.

The old lady with the benevolent face who had welcomed the child with open arms took her into another room serving as a second antechamber. She was brought broth and wine.

"Get warm first," said the lady, in a tone so soft that the child trembled in every limb.

Have you ever heard chickens called in that soft tone, by the cook who has corn in one hand, and a knife in the other? The child, with the precocious experience of a young stray, was frightened by that generosity. Something menacing, like venom, seemed to be hidden in the old woman's throat.

She scarcely dared dampen her lips with the broth; as for the wine, she had the idea of throwing it in the fireplace; she did not dare either to leave it or to drink it.

The old woman left the child alone, in order to go and fetch the mistress of the house; she was only the children's governess.

Who could have suspected that a miserable starveling would neither drink nor eat? Don't little birds open their beaks wide to young tortures who fill them with earth?

Not all, though! There are some who close them; little Ellen was one of that number.

The old woman came back alone. "Lady Lucretia will come down later," she said. "I've been instructed to ask you some questions, my pretty. My name is Amy; I'm the children's governess, you know."

There really were other children in the house, then? That didn't reassure Ellen. Nothing reassured her.

"Where do you come from, darling?"

"I ran away, Madame; I couldn't go back to La Maugrabine; I'd rather be in prison."

"La Maugrabine? Where did you meet her?"

"I'll tell you everything. I met her in Barcelona, a long time ago. At that time she was rich; she took me with her. People called her Señora de Los Amos. Today, she no longer has her beautiful house. We were always traveling. I was frightened of Madame de Los Amos."

"Did she hurt you?"

"She brought Messieurs who frightened me even more than she did, and they talked about selling me—but she never thought the price was high enough. She said that I was her daughter; that wasn't true."

"How did you get away from her, treasure?"

"I ran away. We were in Paris. She wanted to have me taken away by a monsieur with round eyes; he gave her a lot of money, and I heard the coins clinking for a long time while they were being counted; they made a soft noise, like gold."

"Ah! You can tell the difference between the sound of gold and the sound of silver?"

"She's counted so much in front of me, and yet, the more she had, the poorer we were."

"Why, you remind me of Little Red Riding-Hood. You interest me, kitten! Take another glass of wine before you go on."

"I can't drink any more, Madame."

Ellen, aged by the miseries of her young life, sensed that she was caught in a trap. She too was thinking about Little Red Riding-Hood. Perhaps, if she played along, they would take pity on her; the child was fighting with cunning, hoping for the pity of wolves.

She went on, while Madame Amy wiped away the tears that were falling like cold rain from her frightened eyes with a perfumed handkerchief that made her feel drowsy.

"One night, I was alone; La Maugrabine had gone out after counting her money; she'd locked me in. We were living in a little room at the very top of a house; I got out on to the roof; the window of another attic was open, and I got to it.

"There was a young woman in the room, doing needlework. At first she was frightened. I said: 'Let me come in, I beg you; I'm going to fall. I've run away because they wanted to hurt me; I'm afraid."

She came to me and helped me in. She didn't want to send me away. We were both crying.

"I tried to work with her, but I didn't really know how; people only paid for work that was properly done. One day, there was an advertisement in the newspaper for a little girl to do easy things for low pay. I went there; then I was taken to a brasserie, but that wasn't the end of it. A lady with a black face went to search for another, who took me away right away. That one had a face like a mask, which frightened me, under a thick veil that surrounded her black hat. She seemed very old and bent double.

"What scared me was that she had the same voice as La Maugrabine—but I daren't say anything. She took me away right away, telling me that the job as in the country, and, without wanting me to say goodbye to the young woman who had taken me in, she made me get into a railway carriage.

"It was a very long way. At each station I thought we were going to get off, but it was never there. We were alone in first class, with another lady who had a face as hard as a man's.

"Finally, at a station, while I was pretending to be asleep, being too scared, I peeped through my eyelashes and saw the lady arranging her blonde hair—it was a wig, and underneath it was La Maugrabine's grey hair, and she was laughing with the other one.

"I hurled myself outside; the train was moving off; they couldn't get off."

"Aha!" said the woman. "You're not easy to keep caged, my little pigeon. How did you get to London, my lovely?"

"Oh, Madame, have pity on me—don't send me back."

"Don't worry, my love; you won't be sent back. Go on—you interest me greatly."

"I kept going; people didn't notice me. Mademoiselle Mariette had given me a little black dress that was too short for her and an old hat, very plain. I would have been recognized in the vile green dress with the low neckline that I wore in La Maugrabine's house."

"That dress must have made you resemble a rose-bud, treasure."

"Have pity on me, Madame; I've never done any harm to anyone."

"Why, what's frightening you, you silly girl?"

"I don't know."

"Come on, tell me everything."

"I went on like that, asking for work and a little bread in villages, without stopping in towns."

"Aha! You're clever, you know, you little Saint Touch-me-Not?"

"Madame, I beg you, have pity on me; I did no harm by hiding; even a mouse tries to escape from the paws of the cat."

"You're not stupid either, dear heart! Come on, don't be afraid—how did you get to London?"

When I was a long way away, I decided to go into a city; it was Marseilles. I found a little work there; fishermen used me to collect shellfish and repair their nets. I told them what Maman had told me when I was little: that we had our father's family in Ireland. Maman was afraid of those relatives, but I hoped to find them—I don't know why.

"One day, the fishermen said to me: 'Communications between England and Ireland are easy; we're going as far as the English coast; do you want us to take you over the water? It's a bet we've made. We're going all the way around Spain and Portugal—a fine voyage, as you'll see! We'll land in Mount's Bay, where a yachting society will give us a prize—a rosewood boat as big as a clog. It's a big prize that we'll be given as a sign that we've got there in our boat, the *Cannebière*, faster than

165

the frigate *Requin*; we'll also get a branch of red coral mounted on a little stone pedestal on which it says: *Nautical Trial, First Prize*. The *Requin*'s lifting anchor tomorrow; we're leaving at the same time; do you want to me?'

"I was very grateful; they went as far as Mount's Bay with their boat, and left me there, as they'd said, on their way to collect the coral branch and a big green crown that they'd been given, because they'd arrived two hours ahead of the *Requin*, which had only just been sighted at sea when they were already back on the *Cannebière*. It was difficult to leave them, but I was hoping to find Maman.

"They'd given me twenty French francs, after changing them into shillings themselves, and I set off, asking everywhere how I could get to Ireland. I no longer knew how to speak English, but it came back to me, like a dream of the beginning of my life, when I was little."

From the beginning of her life, when she was little! That seemed so far away to her, although it was only twelve years ago.

"Poor thing! Don't worry!"

The old woman wiped the child's tears away again, with the perfumed handkerchief that induced drowsiness.

"Keep the handkerchief, my lovely."

"Oh no, Madame; it's too beautiful. People would think that I've stolen it."

"By the way, you aren't lying, in anything you've said to me?"

"Oh no, Madame; everything I've told you is true."

"Tell me the name of the young woman who took you in, so that we can write to her."

"Mariette Marcel, Madame."

"There's one more question, if you aren't lying. What did you do with the green dress that displeased you so much?"

"I left it in Mariette's apartment, in a box she gave me; she'll surely keep it, in case she sees me again, poor Mariette. I'd rather have burned the vile dress that La Maugrabine was always cutting down a little more at the shoulders."

"You won't regret your frankness."

She was already repenting of having talked about Mariette, but it was too late.

"Here's Madame!" exclaimed the old woman.

Madame? It was Madame de Los Amos, known in Paris as La Maugrabine, in spite of her blonde wig.

The frightened child ran to huddle in the corner of the room.

"There's no point in struggling, you little wretch. I was listening when you talked about me. You can scream, but no one will hear you. You've everything to gain by shutting up and being obedient. Oh, this is how you repay my generosity toward you!" Then, perceiving that the child was suffocating, she added: "You won't come to any harm if you don't resist. Otherwise, you'll be strangled like a sparrow."

"Strangle me!" said the child.

The next day, the Paris police received a letter—anonymous, of course—informing them that the perpetrator of the abduction of the little girl stolen a few months before was one Mariette Marcel, seamstress, of 16 Rue de la Huchette, in whose home a box would be found containing the child's clothing: a green silk robe ornamented with plush of the same color.

Madame de Los Amos was following the method of the man with round eyes.

The seamstress was still living in the same mansard. The little green dress ornamented with plush of the same color, in which poor Ellen looked like a rosebud, was found in the box, as indicated.

The new affair caused a greater stir than the first. It was strange to see a young woman of Mariette's age, with every appearance of honesty, maintaining with such audacity that she had not committed the crime of which they had the proof. Who would not have shivered at such precocious perversity?

"You have to confess," said her own advocate, "or I shall merely be horrified by your duplicity."

Mariette did not confess, and was jailed for five years.

Dr. Gaël followed the case with interest; it was one of the threads for which he was searching. But the threads, broken in the same place, were still floating at random.

The profession followed by Lady Lucretia, otherwise known as Madame de Los Amos or La Maugrabine and a hundred other names, was a luxury trade that put her in contact everywhere with those who could pay for luxury. She had heard mention of the little Ellen, whose family had been searching for her for such a long time.

Now, she had had that little Ellen in her hands, although she had not been aware of the circumstance. Today, she was aware of it; there were two excellent means of procuring a large sum: selling the child, either to the family, who would refrain from asking questions about how she had been found, or to some client like the man with the round eyes. Perhaps it would be possible to do both; it was merely a matter of knowing how to go about it. Was it not necessary to recover her expenses and compensation for the annoyances the child had caused her?

The man with the round eyes had paid her five thousand francs in the House of the Veiled Woman, but he had been obliged to leave Paris, and the little wretch had escaped anyway. This time, she would keep better hold of her.

Like an animal caught in a trap, sensing that the only chance of salvation was to seize on the wing any opportunity that presented itself to flee, Ellen kept quiet, and waited in the echoless room in which she had been locked.

The poor child sensed that she had acted imprudently in telling her whole story, even giving up the name of the woman who had saved her in Paris; she sensed it now that it was too late.

Why had she thought that her mother might have gone back to the relatives of whom she was afraid? Why had she revealed her name? Whichever way the child turned, there was a threat.

Everything scared her, including food. Hunger tortured her, but she dared not eat or drink.

She wasn't allowed a fire, but she wasn't cold; the room was padded like a nest.

Ellen's clothes had been thrown away, and she had been given others; in case of a visit by the family, they were like those worn by little girl everywhere who are brought up under a benevolent sky.

A burning question had been agitating the two collateral branches of the O'Patrick family for some time. Where were the son and his wife?

His two cousins, one of whom had become English while the other had stayed in Ireland, often asked themselves that—but they asked themselves much more frequently were the diamond necklace might be, which made his daughter such a magnificent catch for the class in which inheritances are "prospects."

If the child's death had been certain and the diamonds had been in the hands of Lewis Gray, the head of the English branch, or Jasper Kerry, that would have simplified things—but the diamonds, like the child, had disappeared.

Madame Lucretia searched the newspaper articles related to Ellen and her mother; having found the names of the two branches, she reflected further. There was much at stake.

Ellen was neither blind nor mute. To return the child would be to risk that she would talk much more than was necessary; who could tell whether threats might not be impotent? If, however—which would be better—the past could be given a more appropriate color in her eyes, not selling her would be losing one of those opportunities for gain that one doesn't find twice, and which might develop into an eternal blackmail. The octopus resolved, while awaiting the principal opportunity, to seize in passing any opportunities that chanced to come within range of her tentacles.

There was nothing to prevent her selling Ellen repeatedly, if she could obtain her price. Could she not "repair the damages," as the saying has it?

XV. Erin go Bragh

"Is Patrick related to the O'Patricks? I don't know—and neither does he, or them."

He scarcely bothered about it, especially at present, when, having refused to reinstate a tenant farmer unjustly expelled, he and his sons were accused of belonging to the Moonlight Riders. It was claimed that the two eldest had, while in the process of bargaining, given a miser a spanking over the scales where he had been giving false weight to poor people for twenty years—which did not prevent him from making them pay double the value or from adding usurious interest for the period of the loan.

"Why did they get it there? Because they couldn't get credit elsewhere and the nestlings were hungry."

Nowhere, except in Germany, does one find so many broods hatching, strong and lively, in nests of poverty. Many of those who grow up emigrate; that's why the population of Ireland is declining.

In spite of the large number of births, as in the times of Caesar, it's truly a land of winters.

The O'Patricks and the Patricks were definitely from the same stock. Saying "Patrick" is like saying "Jacques Bonhomme" or "John Bull"—he's the Irish people.

The branch that had grown rich in the depths of time had attached an O to its bonnet like a father; they had long been fond of badges of honor.

Once, the Patricks had been tenant farmers of the O'Patricks; the rich and poor namesakes had lived side by side like that for a long time, the former serving the latter. When the last one had disappeared, the Patricks had still been the tenants of heirs who were waiting for the delay specified by the law in order to appropriate the small piece of land and the ruins of the farm.

Perhaps, by digging, they might find the diamonds, since no one knew where they were. That thought gnawed away at them.

If they had gone to Ireland, the alienists who did not want to hear the story of the execution to the end would have heard talk, like a legend, of the hanged man's diamonds; and also like a legend, in the province of Connaught, sprinkled with large loughs and bitten by profound gulfs, people would have told them that that the body had never been found, and that everyone had long been afraid of the phantom that was to be seen, it was said, wandering in the turloughs that emerged in immense green plains from beneath the water's veil. Of the little farmhouse, ancient among the most ancient, half remained that had escaped the fire; the rest had been rebuilt.

Rows of trees surrounded it, overlooking the meadow; it as from one of those trees that O'Patrick had been hanged, saved by the new crime for which they had come back to fetch the rope. It's rare that a rope brings good fortune to a hanged man, but on this occasion, it had.

It was from that almost-ruin that Jasper Kerry, under the pressure of fear, and in particular, Sir Edward Miry, correspondent of the English section of the International Police came to throw Patrick out—a measure also taken by other landowners under the same influences—although it had always been assumed that he was only occupied in growing potatoes for his master's pigs, oats and barley for their own benefit, and the worst of everything to nourish the tenant's family.

Patrick's family had grown up in ten years and more: his sons, Jem and Joe, laborers, had rebelled, no longer wanting to go hungry while working; even their sister Lucy had been accused of having transmitted a signal by lowering in a certain manner the ragged red hood that she had been wearing during the sixteen years since she had come into the world, having served as a cloak when she was small. It was his friend O'Patrick that had given it to her; she had immediately put it over her shoulders, and now the last shreds formed a hood.

Sally, Patrick's wife, the poor woman, was entirely occupied in looking after her family as best she could. It wasn't easy pretending that she had eaten during the day; the poor woman's lie scarcely stretched the others' share, and restricted her own so much that she scarcely kept herself alive.

Madge, the old mother, had not emerged for three months from the corner in which she lay on the straw. It was also straw that covered her; there was no longer anything else. She was hungry, but she did not want to admit it, in order to increase the share of the three youngest children, Mark, Jack and Jane, who absolutely had to have three meals a day. The two eldest, Jem and Joe, who wanted to eat ever day, were in open revolt. Joe had eaten a raw carrot belonging to the master, and thought he had won a victory.

It wasn't only in Patrick's home that things were like that, for hunger was widespread in Ireland that year—so great that other deprivations that were talked about in families seemed diminished thereby.

Famines, wars, the Elizabethan times when the peasants ate meadow-grass; death when there was no more grass, under Cromwell and the Stuarts, and the House of Orange for a change, and Parliament: everything fell upon Ireland; everything and everyone—and yet, Ireland never admitted that it was beaten; there were white children, upright children, hearts of oak, Fenians and others, emerging from its soil.

While the May roses flowered red in the meadows, like drops of blood, green Erin would not die, the old folk said.

There still existed, a few years ago—and must still exist—a law that permitted a landowner to expel tenants and their families like a flock of wild birds.

They no longer have anything, and no one will give them anything; they wander aimlessly beneath the blind, deaf sky, over the unkind earth, which grows so many crops but has nothing for them. Sometimes, they are deported *en masse* to the English colonies. The measure taken by Jasper Kerry and others precedes and prepares for a deportation.

The night is black; it's raining. The Patricks and two other families of the same kind plunge into the darkness, marching straight ahead; they number about twenty.

Revolution is preceded by terrible repressions; one wonders if their purpose is to provoke it. It is, in the opinion of Sir Edward Miry, a matter of preparing public opinion, as one graves a boat.

Miry is a vile individual, even in matters concerning his own person, without his intending to be. Even his name is not pretty; he did not choose it; the necessity of concealing the accumulation of his crimes led him to adopt the name and identity papers of one of his former friends, whose business affairs he was handling in Paris. Perhaps he had not killed him, but he had concealed his death in order to take over his assets; he possessed hose as well as his papers.

Edward Miry had been an Englishman living in Paris, raised in France and with no legitimate heirs. The man who wears the name of Edward Miry is none other than our old acquaintance the man with the round eyes, who can adopt names and costumes at will, having en entire wardrobe of various biographies and papers. Even the best of them aren't worth very much. If the rogue could get rid of his eyes, he'd be unrecognizable. Fortunately for the fatality that will reckon with him one day, that detail of his person persists beneath all his masks, and the more elegant his blond or white wig is, the more sinister is the fashion in which the cruel eyes shine.

With such a gaze, any vagabond would go straight to the gallows in England. In France, sooner or later, he would receive "Marguerite's cap"[32] in the red arms of the guillotine. But the man with the round eyes lived above the depths where the poor draw out their lives; he was a kind of grandmaster of crime. If suspicions were raised against him he had no lack of people on whom to make the responsibility fall.

It had been time to leave France, however, and he hadn't left any indication behind him, for Julius wasn't dead and he too, under an assumed name—the unfortunate fellow needed one—had not lost sight of his project.

That project was to shed light on his affair, in order to have his place in the sunlight of combat. His convictions, once like a winged stanza, had carried him away

---

[32] *Le chapeau de la Marguerite* was a term once used to refer to a kind of round cap similar to what Americans would call a "beanie." A beheaded individual might, with the aid of a little imagination, seem to be wearing such a cap instead of a head.

without his being aware of it. Julius Borelli, his heart bleeding, had sought a measure of relief by looking forward; he loved the humankind of tomorrow all the more because that of today had broken him cruelly, and, above all, stupidly; indignation and disgust for present stupidities had evolved within him into courage, emerging into the daylight where the Gallic cockerel was beating its wings, crowing the awakening of a new era.

In a novel written under the pseudonym Hermann he had recounted the episode of the brasserie, with assumed names—but there were so many books that, apart from a few naturalists on the lookout for works based in life, no one had paid any attention to it. No one gave any thought any longer to Julius's trial; it had been nearly two years ago. Two years is a long time; there comes a day when people no longer think about people from before that time.

One man alone engraved profoundly in his memory, not merely the book but the place from which it came, Switzerland, and without the necessity of concealing his existence, Julius had immediately paid the price of not being dead, for that one man was the man with the round eyes. He knew henceforth where and under what pseudonym to find the man who had unmasked him—but prudence forbade him to leave Ireland. Even though Edward Miry had always affirmed that he was absolutely the last of his family, and that he had left London at the age of ten, the man with the round eyes had not often strolled through the street of London; he sent his communications regarding the insurrection brooding in the province of Connaught, and the means he had prepared for the deportation, in writing.

Those communications were addressed to the head of the International Police[33] in London.

At the moment when Patrick and his companions were on the move, thrown out of their homes, the man with the round eyes was living in a comfortable house of pleasant appearance in Clew Bay, between the peak of Croagh Patrick, the marvel of Ireland, and Clare Island. It was not the legend of Graine O'Malley, the Sea Queen of Connaught, that sang in his ears; it was the mysterious little clink of gold with which sovereigns, the most suspicious and deceptive race in the world, were paying for the war waged by the man with the round eyes against his enemies—when he had finished looking after himself—while he simultaneously concerned himself with their enemies. Gradually, he acquired the habit of englobing the latter within the former, for the ardor of the chase—an ardor still felt by every human animal—drove him incessantly.

One can imagine, given the savage ardor of the avid human beast—the most passionate of all—how many timid hares were caught in the trap when he went coursing, how many rose up stupidly before the pack. Often, the larger game got away and smaller beasts had their backs broken instead, but that maintains the appetite of the dogs.

The man with the round eyes had become a power all the more terrible because he acted in secret. How many wretches, tracked, banished and ready to be deported *en masse*, could identify the man who had pushed

---

[33] The actual International Criminal Police (Interpol) was not founded until 1923, but it only required a slight stretch of the imagination to envisage some such organization in 1886.

the master? None! It was always like that. Edward Miry was not even known to the agents he employed.

Having simply expelled Patrick and others who were reputed to be fomenting "troubles," forbidding others to come to their aid, Jasper Kerry and others thought they had done enough by way of repression. The man with the round eyes reminded them then that it had become necessary for the general interest and colonial prosperity to remove populations of peasants from Ireland to Australia. Melbourne needed another influx of European workers.

Things moved swiftly. While the exiles were moving in darkness under the rain, carrying the sick and old on stretchers covered with rags, with the little children on their backs, the order arrived to embark them on the *Lough Mask*, departing for Australia.

The armed force, as it is called everywhere, did not arrive quickly enough to take possession of the fugitives, however; they had already taken shelter in the cellars—well-hidden, their entrance being covered with bushes—of the Hibernia Hotel kept by Errigal Donegal, who claimed descend from the first sons of Erin. There, Gaelic is spoken in all its purity, so pleasant to the ear of scholars that the poor inn's dilapidated rooms always contain three or four illustrious guests on their way to visit the twenty isles of Lough Mask, the Giant's Causeway or Croagh Patrick.

Errigal bears the name of an Irish peak, and glories n it.

Two women of modest appearance with lowered hoods—the weather is so cold-have been introduced the fugitives one by one into the narrow opening. Erin go Bragh! They're safe! They're neither the first nor the last to find refuge there.

Inside, they'll be warm; it's rarely cold so far underground, and the two women don't leave them lacking warm soup or potatoes; they'll pay for them later.

The future is dark, but it's not only the *Lough Mask* that can take them overseas, and one after another they'll find passage on other ships; the world is vast.

"Listen," said Patrick, showing them a little box that he has taken out of a leather bag. "Once, a deposit was confined to me; they were diamonds. The man who confided them to me has probably met his final hour; he was a brother, who died for Ireland; if he had lived, he would have given them all in order that a legion of sons of Ireland might be free in some free land; but I can only take two of them; that will be sufficient to pay for the passage and expenses of the twenty of us. Once there, we'll see about preparing a place for the others. It would be an insult to the memory of O'Patrick not to touch the treasure, but it would not be honorable to me to take more of it today. If neither his wife nor his daughter have reappeared in ten years, it's for Ireland."

They all raised their horny hands toward the ceiling, saying in unison: "Erin go Bragh! Ireland forever!"

Patrick returned the little box containing the two diamonds—which were mounted on two sculpted pins in a centuries-old style—to the elder of the two women. "I don't know," he said, "whether Donegal will be able to sell them, but if he doesn't succeed, we'll no longer dare to eat for fear of ruining him, and we won't be able to leave."

"He'll have to," the woman said, simply, as she took the box.

Patrick went back to his mother, who was lying to a mattress at the back of the cellar, lodged in a covert that had often been used for that purpose; the poor woman had just taken a little soup and was trying to warm herself up, following her son's comings and goings in the cellar with her good and simple gaze. She seemed to revive, but the journey had been fatal for her; fever carried her off the following night.

They buried her in the cave, and all of them swore on the poor body that she would remain there. It was one more item to add to Ireland's wrath.

Overhead, in the main room of the inn, Donegal and his wife were examining the dangers and the necessity of selling the diamonds.

"I think I've found a way," said Donegal, finally.

He had, in fact, found one—but he scarcely expected the result.

A few days later, there were numerous travelers at the Hibernia Hotel, a detachment of ten or twelve men employed to scour the region, two scholars in search of antiquities that light cast light on the *fir bolgs* who must, according to legend, have taken possession of the land from an ancient people, who had taken it from another, and so on, until the time when a few human groups, venturing along the coast, had seen the green of the emerald of the seas through the mists.

There were also a couple of travelers, a husband and wife, so well wrapped up that one could only see their eyes; it was so cold in the land of winters.

Another traveler, who was trying to hide his eyes, the only part of him that he had difficulty in disguising, was sitting at a table at the back of the room. As before, in the Brasserie du Bel Escholier, he was correctly dressed and as dinking expensive liquor soberly; and, as before, there was a tall thin man at a nearby table drawing in a sketch-pad.

It was the same scene, transported as if in a dream through time and space—but the correct man was alone, the sketcher had no one with him but his wife, and instead of brasserie girls clad in motley in the French style, two women of humble appearance were circulating in the room, their head covered with Irish hoods, lowered as at the arrival of the fugitives. It appears that, in the telegraphy of peasants, that signifies a permanent danger, so no peasant would approach the Hibernia Hotel unless it was absolutely necessary.

The soldiers drank heartily, extending their hand toward the flames of the fire to warm themselves before resuming the search that they were carrying out in the vicinity.

Suddenly, the traveler whose hat was pulled down over his eyes, turning toward the sketcher, saw the interior of the room—including himself—drawn in a fashion to render its expression (his own was not of a nature to please him). His rapid movement tipped his hat back slightly, and the sketcher saw two round eyes fixed upon him.

In a dark corner, a humble traveler was finishing, on the table where he had just eaten large fuming potatoes with a keen appetite, a letter addressed to Madame Baris, 16 Rue de la Huchette, Paris.

Madame Baris,

I can't give you presenly relible news of the object you hav lost, or rather what you're loking for, I'm infaming myself as I can withot losing corage.

You can rite to me at the Hibenia Hotel at Clew Bay, Conaught (Ireland).

Yor most humble servant,

J***

(followed by the Indian letters).

181

The traveler with the hidden eyes, who had got up and was walking around the room, arrived just in time to see the ma in the corner deposit his finished letter on the table, and as he passed by he read the address.

As chance would have it, the name of Madame Baris was not unknown to him; Dr. Gaël was unaware that his housekeeper, like himself, was often an object of curiosity; he had not thought it imprudent to have letters addressed to her—but then again, does one not arrive at some fatal place as if summoned? The man with the round eyes, the Irishman and his wife were all there, like Jabouille.

The two scholars, who had arrived the previous week in the course of an excursion, were due to spend a fortnight at the Hibernia Hotel, in order to verify for themselves the research of the celebrated Dr. Donegal. They had just come in and had taken their places close to the fire, without letting go of a little suitcase containing a skull—from the era in which Ireland was savage, so they said. Although one could divine from Donegal's smile that he did not think the find was as old as that. He knew, from the legends of his ancestors—all bards of the Gaelic tongue—the fields in which those killed in battle, those buried in cemeteries and those executed were sleeping, and that skull could not be older than the depredations of the Orangists; but he left the scholars their illusion, kindly or mischievously—two of them, perhaps, they were sitting so close to one another. In any case, there are two sides to every question, and Donegal was waiting for them to interrogate him, after having quarreled, before telling them the legend.

The two colleagues, the Hungarian Diderich and the Englishman Tobias, were discussing the probable facial angle of the skull, which one of them had measured placed on the table, the other on a slightly-inclined bracket-table; they were far from being in agreement, and the discussion was beginning to get heated when the hotelier showed them the diamonds, whose antique mounts made them swoon in ecstasy. The skull was forgotten.

They could not afford to purchase diamonds with antique mounts for themselves—they were almost poor—but some museum would surely make the acquisition, which was the same thing.

Diderich opened fire. "Where did you get this treasure, my dear Donegal?" (The hotelier had immediately risen to the rank of those who were dear to him.)

"I got them from a gentleman who inherited them and who, being completely ruined, wants to sell them. I can't name him."

"Can you entrust them to us?"

"To you, I'd gladly confide them; to the adventures that you might encounter, I can't—they don't belong to me."

"Can you come as far as Dublin, to the headquarters of the Committee for Antiquarian Research?"

"I'll go."

"That's good."

The traveler whose drawing had had such a strange effect on the honorable Sir Edward Miry had also risen to his feet, and the two of them met in front of Donegal, who was holding the little box open, replying to the multiple questions of Diderich and Tobias.

The traveler cast a glance at the precious stones, but more particularly at the mounts, recognizable among a thousand. It was an old family heirloom; all the diamonds in the necklace were mounted like that—and before that strange mount, which undoubtedly could not be imitated, the man went frightfully pale, for those diamonds, the heritage of the hanged man, had been among those that he had confided to Patrick, the tenant farmer, twelve years before.

Donegal was sufficiently well-known for the traveler not to have any suspicion of him; he knew Patrick even better; some catastrophe must therefore have occurred in order for him to find that fragment, which could only be on sale for Ireland—which is to say, to save some of its children.

At that moment, O'Patrick—or, if you wish, he caricaturist Odream, the former inmate of the sanitarium—passed close to Jabouille, who had no difficulty recognizing him; he had seen him in his padded cell when he, Jabouille, had gone to the alienist's study.

What! Paris was following him—that commencement frightened him.

Furthermore, Jabouille's voyage of exploration was not going well. But for the calmness of his attitude, the questions he had already asked might have caused him to be mistaken for a spy for some foreign power. Jabouille hoped that, by living in the country for a month or two, he might pick up the trail again.

Fortunately—or unfortunately—he had the famous seal with the two Indian letters, on which he was counting to obtain information "in high places." Jabouille did not lack effrontery—that will save me, he told himself.

The small rooms opening on to the long corridor of the Hibernia Hotel, given to travelers who were staying for some time, were perfectly disposed for the observations of the traveler who was hiding his eyes; his own was connected to the two on either side and to all of them by the corridor along which he slid silently.

Asleep or not, everyone was in their rooms by midnight, in which all of them were pursuing their own trains of thought.

The two antiquarians were measuring the skull in a third position, which changed its aspect completely, and under the influence of the new discovery—the diamonds mounted as they had been several centuries before—and drunk on other antiques, they could not understand where the error in their measurement had come from and were arguing about it bitterly. Everything intoxicates like wine.

The man with the round eyes, leaving the door of his own room ajar, was prowling around the corridor, where he had made a hole in every door with the aid of an exceedingly sharp drill, through which a little light emerged. He applied his eye to the imperceptible openings, taking account of what was keeping his neighbors awake.

That was why, having recognized the caricaturist and being suspicious of Jabouille, he judged it prudent to warn his correspondent that mysterious and extremely dangerous individuals had been sent by secret committees, and that they were lodged in the Hibernia Hotel, where supportive evidence would doubtless be found.

At the same time, he notified Her Majesty's government in London, and then set off for Dublin to issue orders for the arrest of the secret emissaries of international revolutionary groups. He stretched the final words in such a way as to take up a line and a half, which made them seem much more threatening.

The truth is that the man with round eyes was afraid on his own behalf of those who might recognize him, and wanted to be rid of them; so the poor people were his victims and the government his dupe. When the odious measures that he suggested were fatal to them, he would have to make sure that he was underneath at the moment of their fall—that was the only thing about which he was anxious. His life was more important to him than the entire world.

It's a long way from the Hibernia Hotel in Westport, in Connaught, to Dublin, but the railways are not there for nothing; the man could travel anywhere free of charge, and did not deprive himself of the privilege. Sir Edward Miry arrived in Dublin in the afternoon, established his accusation and had the armed force holding the county of Connaught notified by telegraph.

The matter was urgent; the birds might take flight. That's why a considerable detachment invaded Donegal's inn at nightfall. The latter was in the process of making plans with the Hungarian Diderich and the Englishman Tobias to go to Dublin to the headquarters of the Society for Antiquarian Research.

"After all," said Tobias to Diderich, "it's only the mounting that's curious; they might well send Donegal to sell his diamonds elsewhere, if they're too expensive, but we need the mounts in the left-hand display-case in the main hall of the museum."

"We need the mounts," Diderich agree. "The Society will make the sacrifice."

The number of diamonds for sale had increased, because the Irishman and his wife had introduced themselves to Donegal, who had taken them to Patrick, whom they embraced in tears, and the traveler had wanted to add two more diamonds in order that a greater number of the dispossessed would be able to leave.

At the moment when the armed force surrounded the Hibernia Hotel, the Irishman and his wife were in the cellar chatting with the others, telling them about the loss of their children and learning nothing but the constant misfortune of the Emerald Isle, as Donegal always called it.

The four diamonds, according to the arrest reports "must have been stolen from a royal house." The strange seal found on Jabouille, and his refusal to explain its provenance, proved, moreover, that there was a conspiracy. There is often less proof; one doesn't always have a seal bearing Indian letters and diamonds in hand to support allegations.

Jabouille's seal caused the arrest of the two scholars. As there had been a certain alarm when the mysterious letters were found, they had got up from their corner and, looking over the shoulder of the man who was writing the report, quivering, Tobias had said with a smile: "That! It's not thing but the first and last letters of the Indian alphabet, the *a* and the *ksha*."

"I can draw you the other signs," added Diderich, with a similar smile. "It's obvious that the poor man, if he has a mission—which seems impossible to me, in view of his simplicity—only has a scientific mission, so we ought to protect him and it's to us that he ought to explain himself."

"To you and the master," said Jabouille, believing that it would make him safe.

To the scholars, "the master" suggested the idea of a man of immense knowledge. To the policeman, it suggested the idea of a great agitator. The leader of the searchers put his hand on Diderich's shoulder, and even though he appealed to all the academies in Hungary, his arrest and that of Tobias—who appealed to all the scholarly societies in the world—were made immediately.

What would happen, though, if scholars got mixed up in it?

The academies and scholarly societies, however, terrified by the story that ran through Europe, assembled, not to discuss whether they dared to protest of behalf of the two scholars but whether, in the upheaval that might follow, their libraries and collections might be in danger. Even the arrest of the Englishman Tobias was not protested. What were two men compared to so many documents? Even so, they responded to the appeal of their colleagues, with a courage that made their hair stand on end, though: "Tell us frankly, in writing, what happened."

"Don't let them send any letters," said the investigators of the affair.

The inquiry was to be conducted in silence, and Jabouille, Tobias, Diderich and Donegal were to be secretly consigned to prison.

They were to remain there for a long time. The affair, said the man with the round eyes, could not be judged at the present moment without danger.

However, neither the Irishman nor his wife, the two people whose incarceration the man with the round eyes wanted most of all, had been found. He hoped to capture them, though; they could not have left the country.

At the moment when the soldiers arrived, they were in the cave, where Patrick's sons, the cunning Jem and Joe were saying: "Your little boy can only have been hidden by friends of the family; the search they made for poor Ellen might have put them on the track of little James, or he might have talked. You did well to come."

It was almost possible; in any case, it was better to take that route. But who could say that O'Patrick would be safe; there was no limitation on his death sentence if he were considered to be alive, and he had no rights if he were considered to be dead.

While they discussed these questions, the little ones listening with open mouths and wide eyes, Donegal's daughter went past the hole hidden by the bush, where one of the fugitives as incessantly on watch; she had her hood lowered down to her mouth, which signified that no one was to come out; that's why those targeted by the man with the round eyes escaped him that day.

Donegal's wife kept the hotel going courageously, but the story had made a noise and no one dared stay there any longer. If the fugitives didn't lack nourishment, it was because everything the Donegals owned, including clothes and livestock, was gradually sold.

Only one traveler had dared to take a room there, charged by Sir Edward Miry with watching the surroundings and the family. That was why the wife and daughter had not yet been arrested.

The man in question, incessantly on the lookout, inspired too much mistrust for him to be able to discover anything; hazard alone could serve him, and serve then man with the round eyes.

That hazard was O'Patrick's duty to explain the matter of the diamonds. His wife didn't try to stop him; there was nothing to be done against duty. O'Patrick therefore left the exiles' refuge on foot for Dublin, where he arrived without anyone trying to stop him.

"Erin go bragh!" the fugitives had cried, in response to O'Patrick's farewells, and from the threshold of the cave he had replied: "Erin go bragh!"

Dublin, like Ireland, has had many names. It is built on the banks of the Black river, Dubh-Linn, where the daughter of Alpheus is still the black pool of the sea. The Gaels called it Baile atha Cliath, the town of the hurdled ford, and since that time it has never ceased to be one of the poorest cities in Europe—although it is not for those who make it poor.

O'Patrick, stronger, more intelligent and bolder for all the misfortunes that can fall upon one man, went to the Central Court. There, he could not be arrested; that was contrary to legal procedure—so he was arrested the following morning, at the hotel whose address he had given. When he had made his statement, he was sent to Richmond Prison.

Six days later, O'Patrick, summoned to appear before a magistrate, was full of joy on discovering that neither his rationality nor his execution had been called into question—that would avoid any accusation of madness. Moreover, the body never having been recovered and there being no death certificate, he would be considered to be the authentic O'Patrick, with the support of his consequent existence, of which he had given precise details.

"So," the Irishman said to the magistrate, "the innocence of Patrick and the unfortunates who were arrested is established."

"On the contrary, it proves in addition that you, the former insurgent who escaped the final sanction, have not ceased to be in communication with the insurgents of Ireland, to whom you have brought the resources of your fortune. The man who received them is necessarily your accomplice; he has other accomplices himself, in the most dangerous classes of society. An invisible leader—the master—has directed the mysterious conventicles thus far, but he's on the brink of being discovered."

"I had thought," said the astonished O'Patrick, "that you were favorable to the truth."

"To the truth, yes, and, in spite of everything, you may believe that I am on your side. You will realize that when you know that I'm your cousin, Jasper Kerry."

XVI. Julius

There are times when one encounters those who are following the same route, crossroads where men of the same epoch who have passed through the same winnowing-basket are blown by the same wind and heaped up together.

Thus, in this story, thrown from all directions, they arrive twirling in the north wind.

Thus, two contrary motives drove into Westport Bay the man with the round eyes, the representative of international repression, and Julius, the volunteer of the insurrection.

How astonished the latter was to learn about the events at the Hibernia Hotel, and how much greater was his astonishment when he recognized, under the pulled-down hat of Sir Edward Miry, a respectable person entering his hotel holding his niece by the hand, the round eyes he knew so well

Julius was no longer the scatterbrain of old; he was exceedingly careful to avoid attracting his enemy's attention, and, unmistakable as he was, his hair and long beard already gray, enveloped in long and heavy garments, no one had recognized him.

Aided by instinct, however, Sir Edward Miry often turned his eyes in Julius' direction.

"Who is that man?" he asked the hostess.

"A man named Hermann, charged by a editor with drawing the Giant's Causeway, Croagh-Patrick, Clew Bay, Clare Island, Mount Errigal in Donegal—she stood up straight on saying that name, which was that of her family—and all the marvels of Ireland."

The man with the round eyes thought that he did not like sketchers any better than writers,[34] and that he would keep an eye on the man, whose work might be dangerous to the State—which is to say, to him. It was for the safety and vengeance of that man that populations had been sacrificed.

A grave preoccupation prevented him from saying any more that evening, which was that in drawing attention to others he might draw attention to his niece, who was no more reassured than he was, looking around like a frightened bird.

"The child's been frightened," he said to Donegal's wife. "Send our meals up to our room."

That seemed all the more straightforward because the child did not seem ordinary. She must have been raised as if in a box; enveloped in furs, one could scarcely see her eyes; frightened as they were, though, they bore no resemblance to her uncle's round eyes.

In one of the rooms on the corridor with which we're familiar, Sir Edward Miry and his niece were served. A little room for the child adjoined the uncle's room.

While the little girl, drawn by an idea that frightened her, tried to make out the face of the uncle to whom La Maugrabine had recently confided her, the latter, for his part, attempted to reassure her.

"What are you afraid of?"

"I don't know."

"Aren't you glad to have found your uncle?"

"I was always told that I had no uncle, only cousins."

---

[34] The author has apparently forgotten that the man with the round eyes should have recognized the name Hermann.

"That was a lie. Do you know the names of your cousins?"

"There was one that my mother said was very wicked; his name is Jasper Kerry."

The man with the round eyes experienced a slight shock. Madame Lucretia had not told him that she too knew her origin. Who could tell whether she might recognize it someday? But there was no good thinking about that; nothing could be done about it."

He had had her for a week; he would not be running any greater risk by keeping her for a fortnight. In case of an accident, he could get out of it by saying that he had brought Ellen in order to question her more effectively.

Who would dare to suspect him?

Everything that might put someone on the track frightened him, though—including the name Ellen. Why had he let her keep that damnable name? It reminded him of Paris; momentarily, he had a vision of his life while he was there: the various names under which he had committed crime after crime, the little house hidden under the green trees where he had lived alone with his dog, the Brasserie du Bel Escholier, Julius' steely gaze meeting his, searching his mask, and the artist who had just been sent to prison.

At first, he would have given anything for Odream to be captured; now, he would have given anything for him not to have been. The idea of having sent him to prison tormented him.

The rising tide of memory threw up phantoms—but such thoughts did not linger long in the mid of the man with the round eyes.

"Drink, my girl!" he said.

"Thank you, Monsieur."

"Call me Uncle."

"Thank you, Uncle."

Before she could do anything to prevent it, little El-len, enveloped in perfumed scarves that the man took out of a valise—a seemingly sinister valise—was sleeping peacefully.

Julius, certain that he had recognized his man, had gone out into the corridor, and, surprised to find a pre-existent hole in the door, had applied his eye to it.

The man's appearance was correct, but why did he keep his hat pulled down even when he was inside?

It is permissible for everyone to have a timid niece, but when it is the uncle who, in spite of his precautions, makes the niece afraid, that isn't usual. Even so, it doesn't prove anything.

Julius stood there, unable to decide that a man who reminded him of the man with the round eyes might be honest.

The child's sudden drowsiness did not help to dissi-pate his suspicions, but what settled the issue was when Sir Edward, sure that the child could not see him, took off his hat in order to make himself more comfortable, uncovering his round eyes, like a vulture's, avidly fixed on his prey.

Julius was no longer in doubt. He went quietly downstairs and shouted an appeal into the fugitives' cel-lar that no one could fail to heed; "Help! A crime is be-ing committed on the first floor! Come quickly!"

Sir Edward tried to resist, but against so many as-sailants he could not hold out for long. He expected to see one or two men come in, but he found himself in the midst of sixteen; resistance was impossible.

The odious manner in which he had undressed the sleeping child was undeniable, so, caught *in flagrante delicto*, the man with the round eyes weighed up the possibility of flight, recognized its impossibility, for the moment, and wondered how he could put the blame on someone else.

Little Ellen was carried away, still unconscious, into the cellar. Georges, fearfully, was able to observe the unexpected resemblance that the poor little victim would have borne to her daughter, if the dead returned to life.

In the hands of the sixteen sturdy peasants, under the eyes of Julius, whom he had recognized, the man with the round eyes, tightly bound, was led on foot to the nearby village.

"He has to be tried," the fugitives were saying. "We'll allow ourselves to be taken prisoner for that; they'll have to listen to us. All Ireland will rise up."

They were taken prisoner but Ireland did not rise up, for they ran into the detachment of soldiers that as searching the area.

"Help, in the Queen's name, help!" cried Sir Edward Miry, surrounded by the peasants.

The soldiers were armed, and it was one more crime for the rebels to be dragging the honest gentleman violently along in their midst and, in order to excuse their action, accusing him of an abominable crime, when they had designs on his life.

Apart from Julius and two others who escaped, and Patrick's two eldest sons, who were killed, the peasants were taken to the nearby prison. The man with the round eyes gave evidence against them with great skill. He did not know anything about the story of the little girl, he said, and had no idea whether young Ellen would support the slanders of Donegal's wife, whose testimony was invoked and who made accusations against him. That was not surprising, since he had discovered the role played by her husband in the uprising.

All that seemed perfectly true, so the man with the round eyes, whom the bandit had led away in his most indispensable garments, received a thousand apologies, and it was with profound regret for the way in which he had been treated by the insurrection that someone was sent to search for his clothes in order that he could leave suitably dressed.

They search the area thoroughly, but they did not find either the three men who had escaped or the bodies of Jem and Joe Patrick. The latter were buried beside their ancestors, and over them to the vengeance of Ireland was sworn.

Ellen had woken up and recognized her mother; she had told her all about her poor life as a lost child. That would have been a happy occasion, but it was too late; the man with the round eyes had had Ellen for a week, and it was not the first time that he had put her to sleep. It was decided in the cave that Ellen would only be brought forth at the trial, before a crowd that would demand that she speak. Julius too only wanted to come forward in that circumstance, and he was right.

The trial was delayed; neither the man with the round eyes nor the public prosecutor was in any hurry. One was preparing his artillery and the other was afraid of further irritating the crowd.

XVII. The Red-Haired Child Again

While the trial of the Irish "agitators" was in preparation in Ireland, the following item appeared in the French newspapers, with a plea that it be reproduced in the principal papers of the bordering countries:

A child dressed in short trousers, brown gaiters and a Breton jacket disappeared six days ago from the gorse-covered heath near Guérande. The child is small for his age; he is nearly eleven but looks no more than seven. He is recognizable by his bushy hair, red-gold on color. He might have headed for Paris; his name is James and he was adopted by Yves Legonidec, a farmer on the heath, who is in despair since his disappearance. Please address any information on this subject to him immediately.

The child was, indeed, headed for Paris, but the road was long and his legs, although stronger than during his first journey, did not give him a long stride.

For a long time, the poor child had been saying that he wanted to go to Paris to see his mother, and that he would come back. They had let him say it, never thinking that he would actually carry out his plan. His mother had been forced to abandon him when she had been sent to prison; she had no idea where he was, and would probably have gladly left him there. Any information in that regard was considered unnecessary, for now; was he not all right? They could wait.

One day, haunted by the memory of his mother, he set out alone. It was not ingratitude; he loved his adoptive parents almost as much as his mother, but he sensed that she was unhappy, and in his childish naivety, having no notion of how he would do it, he repeated to himself even so: *I shall save her!*

But who would save him? No one.

It was a morning in December; the snow was thick on the ground. He had imagined, by virtue of that bleak winter, that his mother must be even sadder, and he had left, as if to go make snowballs with the other children; he had embraced Yves Legonidec and his young wife, but that often happened, and they had not attached any importance to it.

The other children liked him a great deal, although they had been afraid of him for a long time, believing him to have been brought by the Drak. Now that he had told them about his journeys, they made him tell the story all day long on Sundays, sitting in some sheltered corner. They were no longer afraid.

They day on which he left was a Sunday. Makaïk was the first to become anxious; she had felt that something was amiss since the morning. Then it was Yves Legonidec's turn. He waited until the evening meal, then, no longer able to hold still, stated searching the area.

No one had seen the child. Then they remembered his obsession with Paris. Although many searches were mounted, no one found anything.

"The Drak's taken him back, for sure," said the prophetess.

Makaïk was not far from sharing that idea, as were many others in the locale, even including Yves Legonidec, who had a strong mind. They remembered the child's large thoughtful head, his frail little body and his incessantly-alert intelligence, and the legend took root.

However, the boy's idea of going to Paris simplified the mysterious occurrence.

Especially for a child, there is a world of difference between wandering at hazard and knowing where to go.

Little James had thought about it. He had seen a map of France (a "magnificent illustration" in the Strasbourg *Messager boîteux*,[35] collections of which are conserved in the west, as in the east).

For a long time he searched his route with his finger. When he knew by heart the names of the towns that are placed on a straight line between Finistère and Paris, the child was reassured. The map was not replete with names situated directly between Plogoff, which was not far from the farm, and Paris; there were only four of them: Loudéac, Domfront, Dreux and Versailles.

As for taking the precious map with him, the idea of stealing such a treasure from his adoptive parents never occurred to him.

Twenty paces from the farmhouse James saw Makaïk standing with a poor woman to whom she was giving a large bundle of old clothes. They were both in the open and the north-west wind was blowing harshly; the snow was overflowing their clogs, but they were both so content, like two sisters helping one another, that they did not feel the cold.

Little James loved Makaïk dearly; he began to cry as he walked, but he went on regardless; it was necessary that his mother did not believe him to be dead.

James would be able to pay for his bread on the way; since he had been in the Legonidec house he had

---

[35] *Le Grand Messager boîteux de Strasbourg* was (and still is) an almanac originally published in German, whose French edition was launched in 1814.

been given ten sous every Sunday; a woolen sock had been swollen by them. He had twenty-six francs in ten-sou coins; they were his; he could take them away. But he wouldn't but anything except for a little bread, wanting to keep as much as possible for his mother. Anyway, he wasn't hungry. His heart was heavy because he was leaving the farmhouse.

He had not dared to say anything as he left because they would not have wanted to let him go—but one day Makaïk discovered, scratched with a nail in the fireplace, the word: *I'll come back*—a phrase that the prophetess interpreted in a mysterious fashion, quite convinced that the Drak had carried the child away, and that if he came back, it would be in the form of a phantom, perhaps to bring the Korrigans' gold to farmhouse. It would be necessary to refrain from making use of it before having carried out the conjurations that she would indicate; she had already collected the herbs by moonlight under the oaks of Loz. (She could have spared herself such a long journey.)

The child had not yet reached Plouaret when his legs felt so weary that he could no longer lift the up. Loudéac had seemed so close to Plogoff on the map that he didn't suspect that he wasn't there.

"Isn't this Loudéac, Monsieur?" he asked a man so dark-hued and bizarrely-dressed that he inspired confidence. During his first journey, the child had unconsciously acquired a taste for the picturesque; people and things that were out of the ordinary caught his attention.

"No, my lad, it's Plouaret." The man looked at him interestedly. "Why are you going to Loudéac?"

"To find Maman."

"Is that where she lives?"

"No, but from Loudéac I'll go to Domfront."

"Does she live in Domfront?"

"No, Monsieur."

Then why are you going there?"

"Because from there I'll go further on."

"Where, further on?"

"To Dreux."

"She's in Dreux, then?"

"No."

"Come on, don't tell lies. Why are you going to Dreux?"

"To go to Versailles."

"And from Versailles, where will you go?"

"From Versailles I'll go to Paris."

"So it's in Paris that your mother lives?"

"Yes, Monsieur."

"Why didn't you say that right away?"

"Because I've marked out the stages."

"They're long stages; do you have seven-league boots? Little clown! You can't be as young as you look. Are you seven or twenty?"

"I'm eleven."

"Aren't you growing any longer?"

The tone in which this question was asked frightened the boy, and he replied very swiftly: "Yes, Monsieur, I'm still growing."

"That's a shame—you could make your fortune."

"That's not what I want; I want to see Maman again."

"Do you have money for the journey?"

"Yes, Monsieur."

"That's a shame; I would have offered to take you to Paris. That's where I'm going. I have to be there by New Year's Day."

"Oh, I'd like that. But will it take as long as that if I go on my own?"

"It'll take much longer."

"Then what do I have to do to go with you?"

"Not much. Let yourself be dressed as a savage, and for an hour or two every evening and perform, with a lion that I have over there in that wagon, a drama of my own composition: *The Dwarf Tamer*."

Little James was so cold, had such a strong desire to keep his money intact for his mother, and was so adventurous, the appeal of the unknown being already so powerful in his frail body, that his ardor knew no bounds. He wanted to be introduced to the lion immediately, and his enthusiasm delighted the traveling showman so much that, ten minutes later, he was installed in a vehicle with a poor sick woman, two plump little girls whom he had to save from the lion every evening, and finally, the lion itself, chained to the wall for fear that it might run away—and for no other reason, for the children were asleep between its paws and the poor wild beast, whose sanguinary mores were the main attraction every evening, was resignedly eating bran mash from a bowl, like a big cat. It could have had a little offal for its dessert, but perhaps it preferred the amity with which it was treated—and anyway, when the longing for liberty gripped it, it could roar as much as it wanted, and it had a magnificent *basso profundo*.

The lion was named D'har—an Indian word for conqueror. Its masters had names that were no less strange, although they were simple in the language of their forefathers. The man was Dahawha, the woman Diwha ("man" and "woman" in Sanskrit). The Indians, who had been on the road for thousands of years, father and son, traveling all over the world, were still Indians.

Their twin daughters, born in a village in the Vosges one spring morning were Dyawha, the youth of life, and Ruka, light. That antique-historic poetry, under the influence off continual journeys between big cities, had been slightly shortened into affectionate diminutives; Dyawha had become Aya, Ruka was now only Uya.

The little girls, as plump as skylarks, as hairy as lions, as black-haired as gypsies, created the most charming effect between D'har's paws, and when it carried them off one after the other, during performances, to its lair—made out of pieces of cardboard—the whole barn shook with cheers.[36]

But hunger had finally set in; he found himself going hungry; the cheers having intoxicated him, he dreamed of a true theater and millions, like a prima donna. Dahawha scarcely expected him to come back; he was wondering how long it would take his family to die of starvation when he encountered, to play alongside his magnificent leading role (in fact, it was the lion who was the star), a second major player, smaller and more intelligent than his former dwarf tamer, whom he no longer missed. If James wanted to sign on for a tour, they would see about afterwards.

The woman smiled with joy on seeing little James, as soon as he came into the wagon, immediately set himself between the lion's paws, making a third with her two plump daughters, James' red hair floating in D'har's mane along with the black tresses of Aya and Uya.

---

[36] Some text is obviously missing from the original here, which must have introduced the previous dwarf tamer who is the initial subject of the next paragraph. That paragraph also seems to be incomplete in the original; I have improvised a minimal reconstruction.

Only the lion had dined adequately; it was half asleep, waiting for the performances that no longer arrived.

"Have you brought any bread?" Aya whispered to James. "We aren't performing any longer, and we're hungry."

Young as he was, the child understood that poverty, "Wait!" he said. He was some way from the vehicle when the clown caught up with him. "Running away already?"

"No, I'm looking for supper. I'm the one who can offer it to you; I have money and you're taking me to Paris, so it's only fair."

"Imbecile! Won't your role pay for your journey, and more?" But the man, like the child, had tears in his eyes. "So you want to be one of the family? Wait—I'll go with you."

Together, they went for provisions; the outskirts of the town weren't far away. They brought back bread, frit, and buckwheat crêpes, which made the little girls clap their hands. D'har had two of them. The honest lion licked its lips; it had been a long time since the troupe had had such a feast.

It was like an enchantment. They bedded down in the vehicle at the roadside, and they all slept well.

The next evening, in a barn not far from Loudéac, James made his debut in the role of the dwarf lion-tamer. His hair was dyed back for the occasion and curled, now resembling the hair of a negro child; a bath in a black tincture made up by Dahawha completed the task of rendering him unrecognizable.

The debut was splendid. The little girls graciously allowed themselves to be carried into the cardboard construction that served as a lair; James went into the cave with admirable deliberate stride; roars were heard in the depths of the lair and D'har, who was also a very good actor, reappeared, wrestling with James

The definitive victory was delayed for an appropriate time, and when the dwarf tamer had forced the vanquished lion to lie down at his feet, they went back into the cave and brought out his victims, who danced a fantastic ballet around him, with James, to the sound of a violin with three strings, which Dahawha played perfectly.

The Zingaris, who did not read newspapers, remained utterly unaware of Legonidec's appeal, and the people who watched the performances made no connection between the little black boy and the advertised child with the red hair.

While they progressed toward Paris, where they wanted no arrive by New Year's Day, poverty no longer weighed upon the poor family; its bread was bought with the receipts from performances, and James was no longer counting the days as they drew closer to the capital.

Moving from town to town and village to village, they did indeed arrive in Paris in the final days of December. The theater was set up in Belleville, and the attraction of the drama increased from one night to the next. James gradually built a better understanding with D'har. An immense amity—in which there was a little room for the two dark-skinned girls—bound the boy and the lion together.

Only one thing worried little James: how would his mother recognize him with back skin? Everywhere, it was said that he was a marvel, but he thought that she would like him better as he had been before. After all, though, he had done it in order to see her again, and she wouldn't be annoyed.

It was agreed that James would not leave his friends, after having found his mother, until they had had time to find another dwarf tamer. On arrival in Paris, however much they wanted to keep him, they were honest enough to start searching, according to what James—who could accompany Dahawha without any fear of recognition—could tell them.

Neither the man nor the child, however, simple as they were, had imagined how much curiosity research undertaken by a fairground-performer and a black boy might attract, and how much ranger. As soon as they made their first moves, a circle formed around them at the Brasserie du Bel Escholier.

The lovely Angélique, the widow of a second guillotine-victim—something rarely seen—was at the peak of her glory, more than ever intent on marrying some great name embellished with a large fortune. (There are irrational caprices.) The black La Boulotte had also acquired a share of celebrity at the court of assizes.

As for Frauchen and Rosen, they were still in prison, along with Diana Borelli

"What do you want, my friend?" asked La Boulotte.

"Two glasses of beer."

"Are you going to make your little monkey dance?"

"He doesn't dance; he tames lions."

The circle of idlers closed in around the man and child.

"Where's the lion?"

"Back home, at the house."

"What do you mean, at the house? Do you own one?"

"In the wagon."

"Where can your lion be seen?"

"Every evening, at Belleville."

"At what theater?"

"In a tent at the end of the main street."

"And it's the black boy who goes into the cage?"

"Of course; the lion plays its role with my daughters and Niger." Niger was the name that Dahawha had given little James.

Pestered by the interrogation, the man and the boy wondered how they were ever going to ask a question. They both tried to drink their beer, but James' tears fell into the glass.

"What's up with the little black boy?"

Dahawha had in inspiration. "It's because the first time he came to Paris, a woman cared for him as if he were her own child after we had an accident, and she was employed here."

"Here? What was her name?"

"Hang on...Luisa, I think. Do you remember, child?"

"Yes," said James, stifling his sobs. "Luisa Cardenio, a tall woman with black hair—very beautiful."

"Ha ha! That anthropomorph!" As they pronounced that word they were laughing enough to split their sides. "That anthropomorph, who looks to see whether women are beautiful!"

The man who said that, burbling as he uncovered the rat-like teeth in his mouth, was one of our old acquaintances from the first chapter, the imbecile who was unfolding the copy of the *Totor*.

Another old acquaintance, X***, with whom he had been at odds some time before, is now back in the gang. Vipers don't bite one another. X*** has traveled some distance since then; he has evolved—backwards. Empty after his volume of verse, he had nothing but that in his belly; now look at him, drooling over all the others' works, unable any longer to produce anything but pornographic passages in rags for the use of young and old degenerates

James does not dare to say any more. The black La Boulotte comes to his aid, simultaneously attempting to administer the *coup de grâce*.

"Oh!" she said. "It's Luisa Cardenio—the one who took off. The one who once put on airs like Lady Bountiful, country wench as she was. Well, your beautiful lady's long gone. She's been doing time out at Auberive for a while. She'll have snow on the roof when you see her again!"

As courageous as a man, the child held back his tears and looked at his protector with shiny eyes. He would go to Auberive.

We'll go! thought the brave man. *A trip there's as good as anywhere else.*

Then again, even in that savage there was an egotistic thought, of which he was unashamed, savage that he was: the child would stay with him; the child was a treasure; with that dwarf, intelligent as he was, endowed with a big hairy head and a child's body, there would be years of good pay-days ahead. They would give a few sweeteners to his mother; Dahawha's family would eat every day; the wife was better now, and the girls were almost as big as James. He would make singers of them.

In the meantime, neither the man nor the child dared to ask any more questions. The *coup de grâce* had not yet been delivered, though.

The contributor to the *Totor* took responsibility for that.

"What! Does no one remember any more that Luisa Cardenio escaped, in a black robe and a white head-dress, with all the personnel of Saint-Lazare bowing to her? She's been on the loose for a long time!"

"That's true!" Everyone remembered it.

The child received this new blow squarely in the heart. She had escaped, then, without knowing where her child was, in order to look for him. Who could tell where she had gone? Knowing that she was desperate, alone in the world, he became even sadder, the poor child.

"Why," said X***, good-humoredly, "what's up with your lion-tamer; one might think that he were saying goodbye to the world."

"Nothing's wrong," said little James, pale under his varnish and raising his glass, finding nothing in the depths of his darkening mind but the old refrain sung by his mother, he cried in his shrill dwarf's voice: "Erin go bragh!"

"What did that little monkey say?"

"That gnome," said someone in the group of young pen-pushers.

"It's something from his homeland—some cannibal refrain."

James was furious; there was no doubt about it. The entire population of the café assembled around him.

"Is your lion well-tethered, man?"

"My wagon breaks down into a cage for the whole scene; it's inside with the children and me."

"That's good."

"What time does the curtain go up?"

"Every day from eight in the morning until noon. We rest for two hours then start again until midnight. Every time the performance finishes the public is notified. We have two hours to feed the lion and let the actors rest."

"And what's the price of entrance?"

"Ten centimes—two sous. It's a little expensive, but D'har needs to eat and so do we."

There was a burst of laughter.

"What does your lion eat?"

"A sheep every day."

"Wow! Are you going to make it eat one this evening, in front of us?"

"You can count on us, my man. Until this evening."

The young jokers, glad to have found a cruel and stupid distraction, rubbed their paws together briefly, and dew away, looking back from time to time at the little black boy.

"A fine subject for an anthropological collection—for he'll kick the bucket some day, the winter's so harsh; he'll fetch a good price when his mahout sells his carcass."

"We ought to buy it in advance; it's a fine specimen of the prognathous race."

"No it's not—he's not prognathous."

"Get away! His jaw's dolichocephalic."

"No, it's prognathous."

I say no, I say yes; they argued all the way the entrance where the man with the lion had been standing, but he had disappeared with the negro boy, hoping that they would be forgotten.

When they got back to the theater the child threw himself into Dahawha's arms. "We won't be separated again," he said, "but I need to see my poor mother."

It was, at any rate, very agreeable to Dahawha not to be separated from his dwarf. If they ever found his mother, they would take her with them.

The old woman shed a few tears over the potatoes she distributed all round, from her husband to D'har, who was sitting opposite his image, not reaching out as the others did with his hand covered with paper so as not to soil the potatoes, but opening his mouth as meekly as a dove.

The little girls, hearing words that James never spoke, danced around him and the lion.

Half past two! They had to open up; they were half an hour late.

XVIII. A Grrreat Performance

Some people share with the harpies the privilege of spoiling everything they touch.

Dahawha's drama, with his lion, his black boy and the two dark-skinned girls—who had been getting fatter and fatter since James' arrival as the sous rolled in—was original and attractive.

Civilized woman and primitive man could be seen together.

The stage-set was now almost adequate to create an illusion; the cave was made of better cardboard; it imitated a rock almost as bare as Dahawha's head. The industrious Diwha added moss, lianas and artificial flowers picked up in the streets or bought from stalls. Dyawa and Ruka—the "youth of life" and "light"—were dressed in white cotton wool, their plump dark arms sticking out of that fluffy snow, their long black hair full of coppery sequins, justifying their names.

Even the poster was attractive by virtue of its originality; there was nothing there but the names of the actors, strange as they were; Dahawha regretted not being able to be more prodigal with the patter, but he was proud; his spelling, taken from nature, did not permit him to ruin the impression. As for the names, he knew how to write them—or very nearly. One therefore saw, in large letters always painted by him, with the aid of Diwha, who held the ladder:

THE DWAF TEMER
Melodrama by Dahawa, son of Alif

Characters:

The Lion D'har
The dwaf temer Niger, African nigro
Victims siezed by the lion and singers
Dyawa, Ruka, dancers

Leader of orchestra: Dahawha
Great air roared: D'har
Great air suing: Diwa
Final ballet: all actors

Price of admission: ten sentimes, two sous

Who the Devil can this Dahawa be? Who is this Diwa, these Dyawa and Ruka? All those names set outside the door. But above all, what's a dwaftemer?

"It's a Russian word."

"No, it's a German word."

"Get away! It's English."

Etc., etc.

"As long as D'har and Niger have eaten!"

They came in all the same. The tent was full every time; those going out explained the enigma: it was a *dwarf tamer*. And by dint of two sou coins, the troupe would live; they would surely be sought out by everyone; it was inevitable that James would find his mother.

He thought about that when there were five minutes between performances, while waiting for Dahawha, who was doing his patter, summoning the public to see the show.

They thought they had been spared the young men when a week had gone by, but one day, when all the actors came to show themselves during the summons—

214

except for the lion who contented himself with replying, like the wild beast he was—a passer-by remembered them.

"Until this evening!" he said,

All evening they looked out for the mischievous band of idlers who had threatened to bring D'har a sheep to crunch—an animal which, since having been found dying on the African plain as a cub, had only ever eaten bran mash, the darling!

How would the poor thing cope? He wouldn't want to, poor Keroubim. Keroubim was the pet name they had given him. Perhaps the nasty spectators wouldn't come.

At midnight, Dahawha began to hope that the young jokers had forgotten him. If they came, he would welcome them anyway; when one depends on the public, one can't refuse—but at half past midnight they would close the tent, if they were lucky enough not to have seen them before then.

Midnight…half past! They aren't coming! The entrance is half-closed. D'har is already lying down, curled up in a corner with the children between his paws.

"It's warm in here," say the little girls, pulling the mane over their heads like a hood.

This evening, they won't sleep like that, poor mites; perhaps they'll never sleep there again.

Here come the Messieurs, who have the right to be amused, since they're paying for it. Beware of what might happen; the entire jolly five-strong crowd is drunk; they can hardly stand up, and they're taking up a lot of space. The street is too narrow, for them to stagger there, their heavy heads nodding forward, full of evil ideas.

What can one say? They're paying.

"Hey, lion man, light your candles. He we are, as was promised."

Indeed, the makeshift chandelier was reilluminated. The lion was woken up. James put on his loincloth. The mother enveloped the two big babies with sheets of cotton wool, with the aid of ribbons wound around them, making them white swaddling-clothes not much stranger in form than many fashionable garments, which protect them from the cold of the harsh winter.

The overture began, played on the three-stringed violin by Dahawha.

Then a soft, sad bleating was heard. The messieurs had ordered a sheep to be fetched from the abattoirs at La Villette. The domestic had had a great deal of trouble obtaining one—no one at the abattoir wanted to get out of bed.

For some unknown purpose, the animal had been sheared; the domestic had refused for a long time, but on the observation that it was not worth the trouble of it being woolly to have its throat torn out—and especially because no one wanted to go in search of another—the domestic had brought it.

"Ugh, the nasty creature," he said, striking the sheep's muzzle with his cane as the poor animal shivered with cold.

It would, after all, be more convenient for the lion; he would be able to chew more easily.

"That's what they told me, Monsieur."

"Imbecile!"

In the depths of his cardboard grotto, D'har stretched himself, still half asleep; he was waiting for his cue.

"Well, isn't he saying anything, the damned lion?"

"Prosper, make the animal squeal."

The domestic obeyed. The poor animal emitted a plaintive bleat—but the lion made no response. Like every good actor, he was waiting for the moment to make his entrance.

"He's deaf, your lion—deaf and mute! Perhaps he's made of cardboard!"

D'har emerged at that moment, blinking sleepily. He had missed his entrance! Was he going to have to play for sheep now? he wondered. Perhaps—who could tell?

"It's a mechanical lion!"

"The carnivore's broken!"

"The music-box isn't playing any longer!"

"It's a lion on wheels, for sure!"

"I bet it is!"

"I bet it isn't!"

D'har's enormous stature brought the young jokers' gibes to a halt momentarily.

James, hidden at the back of the stage, heard a hissing sound—the signal for the "roared air."

"Hey, I can hear a snake!"

D'har was about to make up for his entrance; irritated, nervous, perhaps indignant, the poor beast put all that into his leonine throat. Squarely supported on his enormous paws, he turned to the audience like an actor, and then walked along in front of the bars, growling dully, and finally turning to face them, as before, he recommenced a long and profound roar that made the ill-fitted planks tremble.

No one was laughing any longer. Damn! Damn! But the drunks were clinging to their obsession.

"Ah! The time's come for your lion to eat, man! Take him this carcass."

"Pardon, Messieurs; there's a meal in the room, and..."

Poor Dahawha wanted to gain time; he had not enough of diplomacy for that, unfortunately for the poor children.

There are people who would destroy, if they could, all the flowers of May. Fortunately, they cannot destroy the spring that makes the sap swell.

The people too have a red sap, which rises eternally, which makes their daughters so beautiful and their sons so strong. A day will come when that will no longer be for the hecatomb and the market in human flesh.

For them too, Dyawa, the youth of life, and Ruka, light, Youth and Light were made. They were in the shadows, nameless and homeless, swelling the heap of sacrifices, which begins with the caprice of a joker and ends up in the amphitheater.

"Hey, man! Bring out your daughters—they'll have to take the sheep in."

Always obedient to "the public" Dahawha went to fetch his daughters, but he kept them close to him, scenting a further misadventure. They were alone, with five or six young men with a flunkey, who might, if they were discontented, have his tent uprooted the next day, and his lion killed. That had almost happened to him once before. It was in Russia; someone had said that D'har had sniffed the air in the direction of the imperial palace, and if poor Dahawha had not been warned in time, they would all have perished.

They would definitely leave Paris tomorrow; but it was necessary to get through to dawn without any mishap.

The two little girls, not without regret, led away the poor sheep. *Fortunately*, they thought, *D'har won't eat it*.

Indeed, he didn't eat it; the laughter and jeers of the drunken group were so clearly audible in the street that another group—these wearing *trois-ponts* caps[37]—looked into the tent. The band was coming back from an "expedition," some less alert ladies had been collected.

"Hey you! Come in! What are you waiting for? There's nothing for you to do outside. Might as well be in here, in good company."

"Come on, lads, get moving—it's a party!"

They too were drunk. Faced with the little girls padded like buds in winter, pretty with the cotton wool on their chubby bodies, they had a criminal hallucination. Faced with the quivering animal, shaven in the cold and terrified, a thirst for blood took hold of them, as if to staunch the other. Their rage was so great that it could not be sated.

Bloodlust and appetites had them in their grip; they wanted to see the animal's blood run; they wanted to carry off the children and kill them when they had soiled them; they needed all the children in the world.

It is a taste of the blasé Old World, as cannibalism is of people in a primitive state. The beast of prey and desire, the beast whose flesh demands nourishment, was tormenting those creatures, ordinarily so cowardly.

Eyes shining, they delved into their pockets, some for revolvers, others for daggers.

---

[37] *"Trois-pont casquettes"*—unusually capacious caps—were the typical headgear of Parisian pimps at the time.

Have you ever see a pack of wolves before a cornered prey? Many wolves are bitten before a single tooth has touched the prey.

They pressed forward, climbing on top of one another at the bars; the tent reeked of wine and hunting beasts. Each of them, in his own tongue, hurled abuse at the lion.

"Well, are you going to swallow that lamb, you damned lion?"

"It's worthless, my dear—a blind dog, no?"

"Hey, lion man! Hey, dwarf! We need your dog of a lion to bring us the dark girls."

"No, no—it isn't bringing them! Send out the girls! The girls! Let them come alone!"

Increasingly bold in the face of the beast's placidity, they pressed against the bars. One of them bared the blade of his sword-stick and started stabling repeatedly through the bars.

The pricked lion stood up, roaring. The entire band beat a retreat.

The lion's wound was bleeding. The large wild beast, too, was infuriated by the blood—but it was not the ewe that it wanted to punish; D'har had seen where the aggression had come from.

The bars, never being shaken by the docile beast, were only there for the illusion of the spectators. Dahawha trusted his lion, and thus far, he had been right to do so.

This time, in spite of his master's appeal, D'har's roaring shook the bars; the grille collapsed, catching X*** and two of the *trois-pont* caps as if in a trap, whose were stabbed in their turn by thrusts of the lion's claws.

The rest of the band was in full flight. Dahawha, striking Dhar, catching hold of him and pulling him back, did not succeed in making him desist. His claws were red.

The dwarf tamer, whom the beast always obeyed, grabbed the enormous paws and tried to imprison them, in vain.

Blood ran beneath the grille, white X*** and the two *trois-ponts* were choking. Did they deserve that? My God, no.

Suddenly, the lion stopped of his own accord, raised his head, sniffed the air and bounded toward the door.

With the agility of a clown, little James and launched himself on to the back of the animal he could not restrain, and, clinging to his mane like a monkey. Lying on D'har's enormous neck, he allowed himself to be carried away.

James loved D'har too much ever to leave him. He did not leave him now.

From time to time, the beast stopped, looking into the shadows. D'har was following a trail.

The streets are deserted at two o'clock in the morning; they had not encountered anyone when James felt the lion pause, watching two men carrying white packages, sidling along fearfully, on the alert, deprived of one intoxication by the other. The two packages of white cotton wool sparkled under the street-lights.

Just as D'har bounded toward them, a volley of fire knocked him down, along with the child on his back.

A squad of guardians of the peace had thought it appropriate to fire at a lion loose in the streets, which they thought—and everyone, this time, would have agreed with them—might be a danger to public safety.

D'har had fallen, and a further volley put an end to the plaints emerging from the enormous mass lying on the ground—troubled plaints like moans of human agony.

It was the wounded child who had cried out; the beast was inert.

When nothing more was heard, a third volley was fired, as a precaution. Lions often get up again; there were old African hunters there who had scarcely expected to find that prey in Paris.

It did not matter where the lion had escaped from; the first necessity was to clear the public highway. It was while applauding that prompt success that they finally approached the dead lion, and found, on the beast's cadaver, the body of little James, whose blood had washed away the black dye and straightened his red hair.

The men carrying the packets of white cotton wool—those whom the faithful D'har had been pursuing when the bullets had hit him full in the heart—were far away.

Two of the pimps, more rabid than the others, had taken advantage of the opportunity to abduct the poor little girls.

It was thus that Dyawha, the youth of life, and Ruka, light, were thrown while very young to the crows.

A carriage stopped in front of the group that was looking at the lamentable remains of little James under a street light. Two physicians, the alienist and Dr. Gaël, who were on their way to the Gare de Nord, having realized that there had been an accident, could do nothing but certify death.

At the same time, Gaël observed, privately, that beneath the dye on the body and the hair, in the places washed by the warm blood, there was white skin and red-gold hair—the long bushy red hair described by the Irishwoman.

Gaël was almost certain that he was looking at the lost child, the child with the red hair for whom the mother had wanted him to scour the world. One might as well search for a leaf among all those swirling in the wind.

Dr. Gaël gave his address in Dublin, in order that the information that might be discovered in the relation to the sad adventure might be sent to him, and climbed back into the carriage with his brother; they wanted to get there as soon as possible, the trial having commenced.

They were the only ones who could elucidate the matter. Science, they thought, in view of a discovery that might, for one victim sacrificed, save millions, ought not to be guilty of any cowardice.

The information they were sent was brief; no one believed the assertions of Dahawha or those of his wife, accused of having killed, by means of their furious lion, X*** and the three *trois-ponts*, whom the unfortunate fairground artiste had succeeded in extracting from beneath the grille, still breathing but unable to pronounce a word, and who had died while Diwha was seeking help. All the evidence was against them; what they said was false. The little girls they claimed to have been abducted were not found. An anonymous letter accused Dahawha and his wife of having sold them. That charge, added to the accusation of murder, by obliterating any attenuating circumstance, had the mountebank and his wife condemned to death.

Those last descendants of a valiant race had retained their pride, though; they did not want to die before the astonished eyes of the scaffold's idlers; like wild beasts, they wanted to die alone in their lair. Moreover,

Dahawha and Diwha had the ideas of the Brahmins; they imagined that they could follow the track of their daughters when they were delivered from the prison of the flesh, as their legends said.

No one among the dead, however, responds to the cries for help of their family-members in peril.

They poisoned themselves with little pills hidden in the fastenings of their cloaks, ever-ready for such occasions.

The Zoroastrians and the Brahmins are mistaken, like all the rest; the poor children received no more help from the unknown than from unkind society; they were drifting, ever drifting, sad wrecks, with millions of millions of others likewise thrown, very young, into the gutter.

It was years after all this had occurred when two little corpses of brown-skinned girls, cast up by the Seine, were carried to the morgue. Had they thrown themselves in? Perhaps, for the little pieces of copper suspended around their necks like talismans proved that the children had not forgotten the days of their infancy. They were two of the sequins that had glittered in the black hair of Dyawha and Ruka in the beautiful days of the lion D'har and the dwarf tamer.

It was hardly worth the trouble of calling them Youth of Life and Light for them to finish thus! But not everyone in the world has the means to grow up properly, and some pay for others the ransom of the Minotaur.

XIX. The Dublin Trial

Certain things catch the attention, for no apparent reason, at first; but if one digs deeper, one almost always finds them in accord with instinct, as if a kind of odor had alerted us. That was what happened to the editor of the *Revue réaliste*, with regard to the trial in Dublin.

A long time before the first session of the tribunal had revealed to him the immense blunder of the Dublin court, the mysterious affair of the agitators had made X*** wonder—the other X***, the theater critic with whom we're familiar[38]—whether some simple fact that he knew was hidden under all those tenebrous things.

So, spending everything he had, apart from the clothes on his back, to pay for his journey, he arrived at the third hearing. He was very surprised to recognize on the witnesses' bench two men well known to anyone who had the slightest acquaintance with science; Dr. Gaël and the alienist Eraste.

A woman enveloped in a large thick cloak was sitting next to them, and, wrapping herself up for fear of the cold, was wondering whether it was the Devil, in the person of her master, who had brought her here to testi-

---

[38] I have left this passage as it is, because it cannot be repaired by a straightforward substitution; the reader will remember, although the writer and copy-editor clearly do not, that Edmé X***, introduced in the early chapters as the editor of the *Revue réaliste*, was not the theater critic who saw the man with the round eyes at the Théâtre du Palais-Royal, who was named as Marius Rameau, and then as Marcellus, and who emigrated to America after a further accidental run-in with the law.

fy. Bent over by that superstitious terror, she was nevertheless making sure that Dr. Gaël was not exposed to draughts without having the balaclava helmet on his head that he was not conscious of wearing. That was the respectable Madame Basis.

The *Lough Mask* was still in dock; it was thought that she was awaiting the outcome of the trial in order to transport to Australia enough people to populate a valley. When the trial had tipped the balance of public opinion, it would make the rabble of insurgents into a cargo of sturdy lads and lasses to be transported out there, to cultivate the land on behalf of Old Albion.

Summoned by Jasper Kerry, the head of the English branch of the old Irish root-stock of the O'Patricks, old Lewis Gray had come to watch the trial.

A large audience had come to attend that third session along with Lewis Gray, including Patrick's wife and daughter, Sally and Lucy, and Donegal's wife, Ersa—all three of them dragging young Patricks, who were standing on their little legs and watching, in order to remember.

Julius, who was waiting for the time when he wanted to appear, and poor little Ellen and her mother had all come in without being recognized, because they were being sought elsewhere.

Jasper Kerry had recused himself as a magistrate; he was in the audience, beside his relative, Lewis Gray. Both had prepared, for revelation at an opportune moment, an extremely confused clarification.

The first hearing had been devoted to formalities; at the second, the witnesses had begun giving evidence; the soldiers had been heard who had rescued the man with the round eyes and killed two of the bandits. Hired peasants had been heard who claimed to have seen the accused attacking other gentlemen on the roads. They were assuming the proportions of Mandrin's gang.[39]

The audience almost applauded the soldiers, so much intelligence and courage had they deployed in snatching Edward Miry from the brigands.

Then came the deposition of the no-less-brave and no-less-clear-sighted men who had arrested Donegal and cut off the conspiracy at its root, by discovering the signs of emissaries corresponding with the terrible agitator Hermann, thus far undiscoverable. The signs on the seal had to be the password of a conspiracy enveloping the entire world. The diamonds offered for sale by Donegal proved the resources that the conspiracy had at its disposal. The ease with which certain of the accused had hidden demonstrated only too well the how many accomplices it had in the area.

Sir Edward Miry had only appeared briefly—just time to make, in a few words, an exceedingly moderate deposition; the state of his health did not permit him to do more, but he remained at the disposal of the law.

That brief time was enough for Julius' black eyes and the gray eyes of an old man, who had corresponded for twenty years with the real Edward Miry, to fix themselves upon him. The black eyes recognized him and the gray eyes did not—which rendered them more clear-sighted.

The affair might then have taken a disquieting turn for the man with the round eyes if the two men who had just recognized him and failed to recognize him had not

---

[39] Louis Mandrin was a famous 18th century brigand, eventually betrayed by two of his followers, and broken on the wheel.

judged it prudent to defer the clarification that they wanted to provide.

It is probable that anyone who had affirmed opinions contrary to those of the tribunal at that hearing would have been transferred to the dock, all the more so as Dr. Gaël and the alienist, who were in the audience on the witnesses' bench, where they had asked to be placed in order to provide useful enlightenment, were placed under arrest.

The latter had permitted themselves, with regard to the famous seal, to address to their friends the Hungarian Diderich and the Englishmen Tobias one of those smiles employed by scholars who, in the face of certain human stupidities, imagine themselves to be no longer part of humankind, and much less deceived than the rest. They had completely forgotten that what had brought them to the Dublin trial was that they had been badly mistaken themselves in the matter of the supposedly mad artist. But who the Devil could have imagined that Odream really had been executed?

While the smiles exchanged by the four scholars fixed the attention of the tribunal on them, the accused Jabouille was brought in. The latter, looking fearfully from one side of the courtroom to the other, perceived Gaël and the alienist on the witnesses' bench. He stopped dead, wondering if it was really to save a poor devil like him that the two scholar had come from the continent.

Although Jabouille had not pronounced a single word, his physiognomy was clear enough for the tribunal to be able to say: "There's the Master!"

As there were two of them, however, they were both transferred to the dock.

Four scholars! They were involved in it too! What were things coming to, if people like that were also getting mixed up in it, trying to find a lever to hurl the Earth into space?

The depositions continued; Julius was waiting for the man with the round eyes to be recalled, which had happened after the Irishman's response. While the ushers went to look for that respectable witness, the hearing continued.

An abusive speech by the president was addressed to the absent Hermann.

"These are only a few of the instruments," the magistrate said, "of the leader, Hermann, the man who is disturbing the peace of the Irish countryside; the wretched foreigner Hermann is not here to answers; if he dared to present himself, he would be held accountable for the crimes he has caused them to commit."

"You can ask me to account for them!" said Julius, going forward. "The first count is that Sir Edward Miry represented as his niece a poor child bought from a wretch known as Los Amos in Spain, La Maugrabine in France and Madame Lucretia in England. She is the daughter that O'Patrick believed to be dead.

"The second count is that the man who calls himself by that name is either not Edward Miry or was not Monsieur de Gore in Paris; that man has committed crimes everywhere, under all the names he adopts."

"Are you insulting the court?"

"I'm not insulting anyone. I demand liberty for the innocent; do as you wish with the guilty."

The man with the round eyes was introduced at that moment. At the sight of Julius, he looked behind him, seeking to flee, but the crowd was too compact; having no choice, he advanced.

Edward Miry's former correspondent and the former theater critic looked too, anxiously; again one recognized the individual and one did not. In the meantime, the crowd having demanded it, the tribunal had to allow Georges and little Ellen approach.

The phantoms were coming forth now.

Could he not destroy them? No, the people were there.

Can the dead emerge from their tombs? O'Patrick asked himself, for his part. *That really is Ellen.*

The child had to recount the sad circumstances of her life. It was not only her father who recognized her, but the family resemblances were so great that old judge Jasper and Sir Lewis got to their feet to attest that the Irishman and the little girl were their relatives, and the diamonds were the child's inheritance. That would have saddened them if they had not had potential husbands available among their sons.

Were they also accomplices of the agitators, then? One had recused himself, the other came from England but they were supporting the allegations of the accused. That was the question that the members of the tribunal were asking themselves while the man with the round eyes, so pale that he seemed green, tried to laugh at what he called the "insane accusation" for which the crowd wanted him to account.

Then there was a further incident; the former correspondent and the theater critic, astonished to encounter one another in the same movement, having never seen one another before, and who were on opposite sides of the room, came forward, one to say that he knew and the other to say that he did not know the man with the round eyes.

It's a conspiracy! The judges said to themselves, expecting to be massacred in mid-trial. They sent for reinforcements of troops, who merely served to impede the flight of the man with the round eyes. Privately, they compared themselves with Roman senators awaiting the Gauls on their curule seats. Pale and still laughing, the man continued his denials. Julius, defying everyone's vigilance, hurled himself upon the bandit and tore off his blond wig, revealing to everyone the short-cropped back hair that no longer veiled his ferocious round eyes.

The audience began to growl at the delegates of international repression; the session was halted, and everyone, witnesses and accused alike, was detained until the end of the trial at the disposal of the law in the nearest prison, while the tribunal declared itself incompetent and referred the affair to a higher court.

XX. The Wolf in the Fold

On the second evening of his incarceration, the man with the round eyes, driven into a corner by his lies, and about to be convicted of some of his crimes, decided to fight back with audacity. He asked to see one of the judges, whom he knew to be endowed with scant intelligence, and agitated before his eyes the terrible vengeance that the powers whose mandatory he was would take, in response to the persecution undertaken in his regard, and the shame that the judges would feel for having bowed to the pressure of the secret societies of Ireland—the Moonlight Riders and others—so effectively that the old judge was subjugated. He eventually threw his cloak over the shoulders of the man with the round eyes and said: "Come! If you're recognized, I'm doomed, but I want nevertheless to set you free; it's the simplest thing to do."

It was, indeed, the simplest—except that, once outside, the situation became more complicated. One cannot hide as easily in Dublin as in Paris. The man with the round eyes did not allow his guide to do things by halves. "If you don't take me to your home," he said, "I'm doomed."

The other, trembling, obeyed again, and into the bosom of the family of Sir James Claris, the monster was introduced under the damnable title of fugitive.

I'd rather give shelter to all of Ireland in revolt, thought Lady Claris, *than to that man.*

The old judge, for his part, felt his anxiety increasing as the night wore on. He had been seen entering the prison; he had been seen leaving with a man enveloped in his own cloak; had he been noticed? What would happen to him as a result?

In spite of his well-known simplicity, Sir James was now calculating the consequences of his crime. Would he have to answer for it?

How could he, a judge have made such a blunder? He would be accused of it, and, which was even worse for him, already featured in so many popular songs, they would make up a new song, which would run through all the streets. The chorus of the last one was still resounding on everyone's lips: "Get painted on horseback!"[40] As recently as yesterday, he had heard that insolent refrain as he passed by.

Now it would no longer be on horseback that the caricatures would represent him; he would be portrayed escorting an accused man beneath his judge's cloak, and who could tell what they might sing as he passed by? Had he not betrayed the law? How had he come to do it? Yes, how had that come about?

Outside, in the rain, a band of young men had gathered—I have no idea where from—laughing at the fog at life and death with all their ferocious teeth; they thought it would be a good idea, beneath the windows of the famous judge Sir James Claris, to sing an aubade.

The refrain "Get painted on horseback!" had been trailed around the streets for so long that they had had enough of it, and they sounded the morning call with the

---

[40] This line is rendered in English in the original—which does not, alas, make it any more comprehensible. The next chorus, also rendered in English, is more explicit.

233

ballad of the hanged man: "His blackened corpse swings in the air!"[41]

In the state of mind in which Sir James Claris found himself, it would have required much less to make him sweat with fear.

Credulous, simple-minded, impressionable, not at all responsible for the injustices in which he participated, imbued like a sponge with all the prejudices of society—such was the poor man in whose hands human destinies were doomed on an everyday basis. His family had married him off to a rich dowry and a remarkable intelligence, to whom the poor simpleton was attached like a shackle. Often, Lady Claris had prevented her husband's blunders, but she had been unable to anticipate the one he had just committed.

Their daughter Harriet took after her mother; the poor woman had dreaded for a long time that she might go the other way.

Lady Claris experienced nothing but profound pity for her husband; she was pursued by many of his colleagues; they sensed that she was devoid of support, and she was beautiful. In addition to the fact that they disgusted her even more than her husband, though, she had remained honest out of self-respect.

The previous evening, Lady Claris had only said a few words to her husband about the man with the round eyes, and he had not understood; that is why, she went into his room at daybreak, at the very moment when the ballad had caused him to throw his bedclothes over his head like a little child.

---

[41] The author probably has the famous French "Ballade des pendus" by François Villon, in mind, although it would be an unlikely choice for Irish layabouts.

She lifted them off him, also as if he were a child. He smiled joyfully on seeing her.

"James," she said, "I was afraid to talk to you yesterday; you needed to rest; I have to do so today. What do you intend to do with your guest? He's a fugitive; I haven't asked any more than that—but you have to get rid of him for his own sake and ours. Do you hear, James? There's no time to lose."

At first, the old judge had listened to his wife's voice as if it were music. He began to shiver again when he became anxious. So did she.

"Listen, James, that man is neither one of the scientists nor one of the insurgents implicated in the trial. I'll never be able to tell what they might have done. The one you've brought here, I don't need time to judge; that one, James, is a bandit. He mustn't stay here."

He was still listening.

"Make him leave immediately; the glance he cast at our Harriet scared me, and you know, James, that I can see clearly. I don't want us to remain alone with him."

"What can I do?"

"Give him some disguise; give him money—but he has to go, and go quickly."

Someone knocked on the door.

It was the old domestic Mose; rather pale, he informed his master that someone had been sent to fetch him immediately, on behalf of the president of the tribunal.

James Claris left, his legs trembling under his fat belly, as round as a water-skin, where they usually scampered like the paws of a rat.

The man with the round eyes was still in the house!

"Don't leave Harriet's alone today, my dear Mose!" said Lady Claris.

The old man did not need to be told why; he had seen the man with the round eyes come in with his master the previous evening. Unfortunately, his room was distant and he did not think that the peril was so close; he had, however, given the idea of his master bringing such a guest some thought. *Bah! There are honest men who don't look so good—perhaps he was one of those; and Lady Claris is here; she's prudent and knows what's what.*

The man with the round eyes, placed in the most remote apartment in the house, had been able to take note nevertheless of how it was constructed. The place he occupied was like the key to the vault; it gave easy access to the family's rooms, and people rarely bolt their doors as is done in prisons.

The brunette Harriet, taller and stronger than Ellen, was similar in type. The man with the round eyes had seen her beside her mother, when he came in, and had darted the glance at her that had struck Lady Clair as being worthy of an ogre.

The mother and daughter waited for the old judge like that every evening; it was rare for him not to find them awake, chatting by the fireside or reading things that were very distant from the old judge's ideas.

I know full well, he thought, *that they think I'm simple, but they love me as much as if I were intelligent*.

The man with the round eyes experienced no more sympathy for Lady Claris than he had previously experienced for Julius. *I won't stay here long*, he thought, *but before I go, the child won't escape me, as the other one did.*

Once in his room, perfectly safe, his character reappeared in all its hideousness; seething with anger at recent events, lusting after the child, he was in haste to accomplish his crime. The wolf was in the fold; the ogre scented fresh flesh.

The guest-room that had been given to him was one in which the old judge had had put away, in a family writing-desk, certain wads of banknotes reserved for his daughter's dowry –a surprise that he wanted to give her. That would prove to his wife that he was intelligent, he thought. His intelligence did not extend so far as to protect his surprise from bandits that he brought home himself.

The first thing the man with the round eyes did was search the writing-desk; it is in order to be searched that writing-desks are made. He took the wads of cash and stuffed them in his pockets and in the lining of a black coat that he put on instead of his own. After covering it with a second coat, he sat down for a few minutes.

Everyone ought to be asleep, but how was he going to find his way? How would he get to the child? First, a wolf tears out the throats of the entire flock, and then thinks about escaping. The man with the round eyes was superior to a wolf in one respect—that of first obtaining what he needed for his own security. Now he could act decisively; he had made a note of the door to Harriet's room; it connected to that of Lady Claris. Until morning, he kept watch. He needed the child, and destiny was on his side!

At daybreak, when Lady Claris went to see her husband, the man with the round eyes crept to the door of her room; it was empty; he was easily able to reach Harriet's. By the uncertain dawn light, he saw her as through a veil.

The child was surrounded by everything that might develop her intelligence—as all the children of the human race will be one day. She had fallen asleep while reading.

The book had fallen to the floor. It was a serious book that people of her age like passionately: Darwin. Lady Claris did not keep her daughter in ignorance of any of the questions that, once presented scientifically, become appropriate and no longer affect the imagination. They are as simple as the seeds from which flowers will grow.

On the piano there was a little of everything: songs of the old days, recent works, ballads in Gaelic, extracts from the old masters. The child loved Wagner; she sensed something in birth in those monstrous choirs, and, dreamily seeking on her guitar the intervals between the intervals, she found the voice of the wind, and beyond the scales of the wind, yet other scales.

As the tongues that rivers divide from the same source will fall back into the same ocean, the music of the tongue of the human race, melted into mere dialects, is returning by degrees toward the common ocean. Like every young artiste, Harriet, always going forward, would not have to travel for long.

On her bedside table there was a little painting, broadly sketched out, a simple moonlight scene in which the intermediary shades passed through all the shades of gray, allowing large white gleams to float here and there.

At first, the man with the round eyes was afraid of that painting, of the white gleams floating there like spectral forms. Then that impression made him laugh. Another idea occurred to him. What if the mother were to come back?

Before the sleeping child, however, the appetite of the ogre overwhelmed him; he forgot everything else.

On the floor there were balls of wool and over-turned baskets; a family pet had been frolicking there.

He remembered the little dog in the brasserie. In passing from one owner to another and animal might go far. Who could tell whether his enemy might suddenly appear in front of him?

That made him laugh again: his crocodile laugh, which uncovered pointed teeth.

An opening hollowed out beneath the wallpaper at the back of the room reassured him; it was a cat that was able to enter and leave freely. But where did the cat-flap lead? What did it matter? Only a cat could get through it.

Avidly, he approached the bed; her head sunk into her white billow, her long hair hanging loose, the child, who had stayed up late, was profoundly asleep.

No chloroform! She might scream—but what did it matter? The human beast pounced.

Harriet was indeed about to scream, but the two ter-rible hands of the man with the round eyes—two enor-mous, hairy hands, which he always hid inside gloves because they reminded people of a gorilla's paws; the claws of a monster—closed around the child's neck. Harriet did not scream; nor did she submit to the mon-ster's outrages alive. Harriet was dead.

Every morning it was her mother who woke her up when it was broad daylight. Her big gray cat came in first, when it had not spent the night on Harriet's bed. This time, Pussy had been dreaming on the roof in the moonlight; he suddenly came back in. The man with the round eyes heard a roar of rage; Frightened, he ran for the door, and as he opened it he looked back to see the cat moaning and wailing over the child's body.

Audacity might save him; the man with the round eyes wanted to flee without delay. Now he was thinking about his safety. He would calmly leave the house, and once outside, would take the most deserted streets. He would throw his outer coat into the first available hole and go in the other to the nearest railway station; had he not fled many times already?

Composing his features, he took the corridor leading to the drawing room where he found Lady Claris and the old domestic.

"I've realized," said the man with the round eyes, "that my presence here might attract trouble, so I'm leaving."

Without replying, the mother watched him go out, and then took fright. Followed by the old man, she ran to Harriet's room. It was too late.

The cat, ceasing to moan, sniffed the air like a dog and hurtled through the open door.

When felines take it upon themselves to love someone, it is for life; that was how poor Pussy loved his young mistress.

By his own route he reached the staircase.

The man with the round eyes went quickly down the stone stairs of the old house, but not quickly enough for the cat to be able to catch up with him and follow him, growling.

Alarmed by the cries of fury he could hear behind him, the wretch, instead of going out into the street, turned toward a cellar whose spiral stairway opened nearby. The pause that he made to get his bewaring gave the cat time to leap at his face, his claws scoring the monster's round eyes.

The man started running recklessly down the steps of the spiral stairway but stumbled, and fell to the bottom, the cat still clamped on to his face. The fall was a bad one.

Only the spine of the man with the round eyes was unbroken by the fall; he was alive, feeling his broken arms and legs like inert masses weighing him down.

Then the vengeful beast, the cat, which had followed him in his tumble, dragged itself toward him, with its back broken, and used the last effort of its agony to bite into his throat.

Because the wretch was unable to move, that continued for hours.

When Pussy lay down, with one last miaow, the man with the round eyes was blind and his neck was horrible lacerated, shedding rivulets of blood.

In old buildings in Dublin, as in London and Paris, the sewers beneath the cellars are inhabited by legions of rats. One might think that they were squirrels, so gracefully do they make use of their tiny rodent hands. Sometimes, one is surprised by the resemblance that they have to certain monkeys, and their intelligence, enveloped by the war against humankind, does not lag behind that of any other animal.

In old neighborhoods, there are venerable rats white with age, which, it is said, the young ones guide and warn about danger; those of middle age have a coarse appearance; the very young, wild beasts with long hair, would be charming creatures if it were not for the long tail, always dirty, which every authentic rat trails behind it like a fat worm.

These rats are ferocious, not eating every day and perhaps being aware of the needless cruelties exercised upon them before killing them. Who knows whether those that escape might not tell tales?

That day, for the rats inhabiting the judge's cellars, there was a joyous feast. It lasted a long time—swarming, fighting epic battles and stuffing themselves, without anyone coming to disturb them. No one even spared a thought for the cellar where they were banqueting.

When the carcass of the cat had been devoured, it took them an entire day to eat the living wretch who, with his arms and legs broken, could not make a movement.

Sir James Claris came back delighted by the escape of the man with the round eyes, which had avoided formidable difficulties and which had almost won him an ovation at the Central Court.

He went back into his house at a run, and discovered there what his guest had done.

The trial of the agitators was stifled; the four scientists, returned to the societies that petitioned for their release, had formal instructions not to talk about the matter, and as there was no scientific question at stake, they resigned themselves to keep quiet.

Julius and the others had to wait for another hearing; his case had been separated completely from that of the Irishmen caught in the act of ill-treating a man on a secret mission. Donegal, who had given them shelter, remained in prison with them. His wife and daughter returned to the little hotel, where, still as secretly, the children of Erin, white children, boycotters, Moonlight Riders and tenant farmers tracked like wild beasts, found shelter.

The four scientists protested on behalf of the prisoners in the name of all the academies on the world, but the judges in Dublin remained deaf.

One night, however, someone came to fetch the prisoners, and they thought they were free, when they perceived in the harbor to which they had been taken, the launches of the *Lough Mask*, already loaded with their families. Their deportation had been "deemed necessary," and that was what they got.

On the ship, a woman wearing full mourning came to join them.

"I shall care for you," she said, "and I shall help to raise your children; I too have been subjected to the same fatalities as you. It was Harriet's mother, who had been unable to survive the desolation of her hearth.

The two branches of the O'Patrick family had wanted to set things in motion to delay his deportation, and especially that of the diamonds, but they ceased their efforts, saying sadly: "Ellen won't ever marry; it's obvious that she'll soon die.

In fact, she died during the crossing. Her child's body was consigned in a shroud to the waves.

Madame Lucretia had disappeared. Are vipers of that sort ever caught? Under another name, she founded an "educational establishment" for young maidens. Perhaps one of the children sold as animals will set fire to it, for no other justice will pass that way.

XXI. Diana Borelli

Do you think that those two women—Diana Borelli, who had committed no sin, and that poor old mother with a face so aged by dolor that it was like a crescent moon,[42] whom we met in the early chapters—were not honest, beneath their numbers of infamy? Was it not better for the latter to kill her child than to let her drag herself through the streets beneath her shame?

There are many others in prisons who are honest. As for the others, whose is the sin?

They were released on the same day, the old woman by death, the other by the hazard of a name similar to her own: Diana Boveli. She was a young woman of great beauty, guilty of some fraud or other to furnish her wardrobe, for whom great fortunes obtained a pardon. The files were mixed up; it was Diana Borelli who was set free, and once the pardon was granted, Diana Boveli's protectors preferred to solicit a second one rather than attract attention to themselves by pointing out the mistake.

Diana Borelli left for Australia, from which she escaped with her brother Julius. Julius wanted to found, in some location belonging only to nature—whether in the glacial solitudes of the poles or the profound forests of Africa, in some primitive place where only the valiant ever came—a colony of people who, weary of the evil

---

[42] The author has evidently forgotten that it was the religious confidence trickster, not the woman who had killed her daughter, who was described in the earlier chapter as having a face "like a crescent moon."

that had been done to them, would turn the instinct of struggle against nature, and perhaps with be the root of a race in which the rudiments of the most beautiful things—justice, liberty and science—would no longer be perverted, and which would enlighten the humankind of tomorrow.

Dr. Gaël is thinking about going to join Julius, and perhaps he will; that thought terrifies Madame Basis, who dreads long journeys, but she will follow him all the same.

Jabouille summoned his wife and children to Australia, and swears that he will never go to sea any further than Melbourne harbor—but who knows? Destiny is strange.

The Irishman O'Patrick and his wife have set off to find Julius; they have written to Dr. Gaël, and perhaps that will convince him to make the voyage.

They are in the same place to which the whaler Josiah had taken Olaff, for the Russian, Olaff's friend, had talked about the projected voyage to Julius. What attracts Dr. Gaël is the submarine prairies full of monsters of species that once disappeared; it is the geological torments that eat into the shores and disembowel mountains, uncovering mines that would give the old world a larger banquet of life but, more importantly, might perhaps reveal unknown metals, and entire animals conserved by the ice, witnesses to vanishes ages.

Who knows of what Gaël dreams? Who knows what might become of the colony that will also be joined by the Donegal family?

Who, knows, O new legend, whether one your epics might not be lived and sung there?

SF & FANTASY

Henri Allorge. *The Great Cataclysm*
Guy d'Armen. *Doc Ardan: The City of Gold and Lepers*
G.-J. Arnaud. *The Ice Company*
Charles Asselineau. *The Double Life*
Cyprien Bérard. *The Vampire Lord Ruthwen*
Aloysius Bertrand. *Gaspard de la Nuit*
Richard Bessière. *The Gardens of the Apocalypse*
Albert Bleunard. *Ever Smaller*
Félix Bodin. *The Novel of the Future*
Alphonse Brown. *City of Glass*
André Caroff. *The Terror of Madame Atomos; Miss Atomos; The Return of Madame Atomos; The Mistake of Madame Atomos; The Monsters of Madame Atomos*
Félicien Champsaur. *The Human Arrow; Ouha*
Didier de Chousy. *Ignis*
Captain Danrit. *Undersea Odyssey*
C. I. Defontenay. *Star (Psi Cassiopeia)*
Charles Derennes. *The People of the Pole*
Georges Dodds (anthologist). *The Missing Link*
Harry Dickson. *The Heir of Dracula*
Jules Dornay. *Lord Ruthven Begins*
Alfred Driou. *The Adventures of a Parisian Aeronaut*
Sâr Dubnotal *vs. Jack the Ripper*
Alexandre Dumas. *The Return of Lord Ruthven*
Renée Dunan. *Baal*
J.-C. Dunyach. *The Night Orchid; The Thieves of Silence*
Henri Duvernois. *The Man Who Found Himself*
Achille Eyraud. *Voyage to Venus*
Henri Falk. *The Age of Lead*
Paul Féval. *Anne of the Isles; Knightshade; Revenants; Vampire City; The Vampire Countess; The Wandering Jew's Daughter*
Paul Féval, *fils. Felifax, the Tiger-Man*
Charles de Fieux. *Lamékis*
Arnould Galopin. *Doctor Omega; Doctor Omega & The Shadowmen*
G.L. Gick. *Harry Dickson and the Werewolf of Rutherford Grange*
Edmond Haraucourt. *Illusions of Immortality*
Nathalie Henneberg. *The Green Gods*
V. Hugo, P. Foucher & P. Meurice. *The Hunchback of Notre-Dame*

Michel Jeury. *Chronolysis*
Gustave Kahn. *The Tale of Gold and Silence*
Gérard Klein. *The Mote in Time's Eye*
Jean de La Hire. *Enter the Nyctalope; The Nyctalope on Mars; The Nyctalope vs. Lucifer; The Nyctalope Steps In; Night of the Nyctalope*
Etienne-Léon de Lamothe-Langon. *The Virgin Vampire*
André Laurie. *Spiridon*
Gabriel de Lautrec. *The Vengeance of the Oval Portrait*
Alain le Drimeur. *The Future City*
Georges Le Faure & Henri de Graffigny. *The Extraordinary Adventures of a Russian Scientist Across the Solar System* (2 vols.)
Gustave Le Rouge. *The Vampires of Mars The Dominion of the World* (w/Gustave Guitton) (4 vols.)
Jules Lermina. *Mysteryville; Panic in Paris; To-Ho and the Gold Destroyers; The Secret of Zippelius*
Jean-Marc & Randy Lofficier. *Edgar Allan Poe on Mars; The Katrina Protocol; Pacifica; Robonocchio; Tales of the Shadowmen 1-8*
Xavier Mauméjean. *The League of Heroes*
Joseph Méry. *The Tower of Destiny*
Hippolyte Mettais. *The Year 5865*
Louise Michel. *The Human Microbes; The New World*
José Moselli. *Illa's End*
John-Antoine Nau. *Enemy Force*
Marie Nizet. *Captain Vampire*
C. Nodier, A. Beraud & Toussaint-Merle. *Frankenstein*
Henri de Parville. *An Inhabitant of the Planet Mars*
Gaston de Pawlowski. *Journey to the Land of the 4th Dimension*
Georges Pellerin. *The World in 2000 Years*
Pierre Pelot. *The Child Who Walked on the Sky*
J. Polidori, C. Nodier, E. Scribe. *Lord Ruthven the Vampire*
P.-A. Ponson du Terrail. *The Vampire and the Devil's Son*
Henri de Régnier. *A Surfeit of Mirrors*
Maurice Renard. *The Blue Peril; Doctor Lerne; The Doctored Man; A Man Among the Microbes; The Master of Light*
Jean Richepin. *The Wing*
Albert Robida. *The Adventures of Saturnin Farandoul; The Clock of the Centuries; Chalet in the Sky*
J.-H. Rosny Aîné. *Helgvor of the Blue River; The Givreuse Enigma; The Mysterious Force; The Navigators of Space; Vamireh; The World of the Variants; The Young Vampire*
Marcel Rouff. *Journey to the Inverted World*

Han Ryner. *The Superhumans*

Brian Stableford. *The New Faust at the Tragicomique; The Empire of the Necromancers (The Shadow of Frankenstein; Frankenstein and the Vampire Countess; Frankenstein in London); Sherlock Holmes & The Vampires of Eternity; The Stones of Camelot; The Wayward Muse.* (anthologist) *The Germans on Venus; News from the Moon; The Supreme Progress; The World Above the World; Nemoville; Investigations of the Future*

Jacques Spitz. *The Eye of Purgatory*

Kurt Steiner. *Ortog*

Eugène Thébault. *Radio-Terror*

C.-F. Tiphaigne de La Roche. *Amilec*

Théo Varlet. *The Xenobiotic Invasion; Timeslip Troopers* (w/André Blandin); *The Martian Epic* (w/Octave Joncquel)

Paul Vibert. *The Mysterious Fluid*

Villiers de l'Isle-Adam. *The Scaffold; The Vampire Soul*

Philippe Ward. *Artahe*

Philippe Ward & Sylvie Miller. *The Song of Montségur*

MYSTERIES & THRILLERS

M. Allain & P. Souvestre. *The Daughter of Fantômas*

A. Anicet-Bourgeois, Lucien Dabril. *Rocambole*

A. Bernède. *Belphegor; Judex* (w/Louis Feuillade)

A. Bisson & G. Livet. *Nick Carter vs. Fantômas*

V. Darlay & H. de Gorsse. *Lupin vs. Holmes: The Stage Play*

Paul Féval. *Gentlemen of the Night; John Devil; The Black Coats ('Salem Street; The Invisible Weapon; The Parisian Jungle; The Companions of the Treasure; Heart of Steel; The Cadet Gang; The Sword-Swallower)*

Emile Gaboriau. *Monsieur Lecoq*

Steve Leadley. *Sherlock Holmes: The Circle of Blood*

Maurice Leblanc. *Arsène Lupin vs. Countess Cagliostro; Lupin vs. Holmes (The Blonde Phantom; The Hollow Needle); The Many Faces of Arsène Lupin*

Gaston Leroux. *Chéri-Bibi; The Phantom of the Opera; Rouletabille & the Mystery of the Yellow Room*

Richard Marsh. *The Complete Adventures of Judith Lee*

William Patrick Maynard. *The Terror of Fu Manchu; The Destiny of Fu Manchu*

Frank J. Morlock. *Sherlock Holmes: The Grand Horizontals; Sherlock Holmes vs Jack the Ripper*
Antonin Reschal. *The Adventures of Miss Boston*
P. de Wattyne & Y. Walter. *Sherlock Holmes vs. Fantômas*
David White. *Fantômas in America*

SCREENPLAYS

Mike Baron. *The Iron Triangle*
Emma Bull & Will Shetterly. *Nightspeeder; War for the Oaks*
Gerry Conway & Roy Thomas. *Doc Dynamo*
Steve Englehart. *Majorca*
James Hudnall. *The Devastator*
Jean-Marc & Randy Lofficier. *Royal Flush*
J.-M. & R. Lofficier & Marc Agapit. *Despair*
J.-M. & R. Lofficier & Joël Houssin. *City*
Andrew Paquette. *Peripheral Vision*
Robert L. Robinson, Jr. *Judex*
R. Thomas, J. Hendler & L. Sprague de Camp. *Rivers of Time*

NON-FICTION

Stephen R. Bissette. *Blur 1-5. Green Mountain Cinema 1; Teen Angels*
Win Scott Eckert. *Crossovers* (2 vols.)
Jean-Marc & Randy Lofficier. *Shadowmen* (2 vols.)
Randy Lofficier. *Over Here*

HEXAGON COMICS

Franco Frescura & Luciano Bernasconi. *Wampus*
Franco Frescura & Giorgio Trevisan. *CLASH*
L. Bernasconi, J.-M. Lofficier & Juan Roncagliolo Berger. *Phenix*
Claude Legrand, J.-M. Lofficier & L. Bernasconi. *Kabur*
Franco Oneta. *Zembla*
L. Buffolente, Lofficier & J.-J. Dzialowski. *Strangers: Homicron*
Danilo Grossi. *Strangers: Jaydee*
Claude Legrand & Luciano Bernasconi. *Strangers: Starlock*

ART BOOKS

Jean-Pierre Normand. *Science Fiction Illustrations*
Raven Okeefe. *Raven's L'il Critters; Rave's Faves*
Randy Lofficier & Raven Okeefe. *If Your Possum Go Daylight...*
Daniele Serra. *Illusions*